RIBBY'S SECRET

Cathy McGough

Stratford Living Publishing

Copyright © 2015 by Cathy McGough
All rights reserved.
This updated version published in September, 2024.
No portion of this book may be reproduced in any form without written permission from the publisher or author, except as permitted by U.S. copyright law without prior permission in writing from the Publisher at Stratford Living Publishing.
ISBN PAPERBACK: 978-1-998480-47-0
ISBN ebook: 978-1-998480-48-7
Cathy McGough has asserted her right under the Copyright, Designs and Patents Act, 1988 to be identified as the author of this work.
Cover art powered by Canva Pro.
This is a work of fiction. The characters and situations are all fictional. Resemblance to any persons living or dead is purely coincidental. Names, characters, places, and incidents are either the products of the author's imagination or are used fictiously.

WHAT READERS ARE SAYING

US:

"The whole story is sweet at times, but most of the time it is terrifying. The author has an interesting way of telling a story and made this book highly entertaining."

"Like Bernheimer, McGough's style of storytelling might not be for everyone. There's a good amount of suspension of disbelief that has to happen in order to accept Angela's presence and several events and situations in the plot. I believe the effort is worth the time. I'm looking forward to exploring more of this author's work."

"An enjoyable and disturbing read and it delivered on the promise of being a psychological domestic thriller."

"A dark, psychological thriller that will have you sitting on the edge of your seat and refusing to put it down until you have reached the end!"

"Wow! What a ride this one was! The way this tale is told will leave you wondering what just happened to you."

"This is a full-on psycho-biddy women's horror story, told with dry humour."

UK:

"Ribby holds so many secrets. A lovely but sad story."

"Ribby's Secret is both an interesting and enjoyable, yet disturbing on many levels and is well worth the read."

"Well written with compelling characters and an intriguing journey."

Contents

Epigraph	XI
Dedication	XIII
POEM: ON THE SURFACE	XV
Prologue	XVII
Chapter One	1
***	7
***	11
***	16
Chapter Two	19
***	22
Chapter Three	28
***	33
Chapter Four	36
Chapter Five	39
Chapter Six	42
***	44

***	51
Chapter Seven	56
Chapter Eight	59
Chapter Nine	65
***	67
***	69
Chapter Ten	71
Chapter Eleven	75
***	78
Chapter Twelve	81
***	83
Chapter Thirteen	87
Chapter Fourteen	91
Chapter Fifteen	93
Chapter Sixteen	96
***	99
***	102
Chapter Seventeen	107
***	110
Chapter Eighteen	112
Chapter Nineteen	115

***	119
Chapter Twenty	121
Chapter Twenty-One	124
Chapter Twenty-Two	127
Chapter Twenty-Three	131
Chapter Twenty-Four	135
***	139
Chapter Twenty-Five	140
Chapter Twenty-Six	144
***	147
Chapter Twenty-Seven	158
***	163
***	165
Chapter Twenty-Eight	167
Chapter Twenty-Nine	174
***	178
Chapter Thirty	183
Chapter Thirty-One	188
Chapter Thirty-Two	190
Chapter Thirty-Three	193
***	197

Chapter Thirty-Four	200
Chapter Thirty-Five	204
Chapter Thirty-Six	207
Chapter Thirty-Seven	210
***	212
***	214
Chapter Thirty-Eight	216
Chapter Thirty-Nine	219
Chapter Forty	221
Chapter Forty-One	224
***	228
Chapter Forty-Two	229
***	231
Chapter Forty-Three	232
Chapter Forty-Four	233
Chapter Forty-Five	235
Chapter Forty-Six	237
Chapter Forty-Seven	238
Chapter Forty-Eight	241
***	243
***	246

Chapter Forty-Nine	248
Chapter Fifty	250
Chapter Fifty-One	256
Chapter Fifty-Two	259
***	261
Chapter Fifty-Three	263
Chapter Fifty-Four	267
***	268
***	270
Chapter Fifty-Five	271
***	273
Chapter Fifty-Six	276
Chapter Fifty-Seven	279
Chapter Fifty-Eight	284
Chapter Fifty-Nine	286
Chapter Sixty	287
***	290
Chapter Sixty-One	292
Chapter Sixty-Two	297
Chapter Sixty-Three	301
Chapter Sixty-Four	302

Chapter Sixty-Five	305
***	306
Chapter Sixty-Six	311
Chapter Sixty-Seven	314
***	315
Chapter Sixty-Eight	316
Chapter Sixty-Nine	318
Chapter Seventy	322
Chapter Seventy-One	328
Chapter Seventy-Two	331
Chapter Seventy-Three	333
***	335
***	337
***	341
Epilogue	343
Quote	345
Word From The Author	347
About The Author	349
Also by:	351

"My secrets cry aloud.

I have no need for tongue.

My heart keeps open house,

My doors are widely flung."

Theodore Roethke

For Imaginary Friends and Those Who Need Them

POEM: ON THE SURFACE

Copyright © 2014 by Cathy McGough
Mirror,
You reflect
me with redundancy
Written all
over me
Is flesh
coloured uncertainty.
Mirror,
You mock
perfection
With this refrained
reflection
And the
result is always the same
In your
frame: I remain unchanged.
Written
between the lines
Disguised
poetically

Inescapable
features
Flow
inharmoniously.
Mirror: I
adhere to what I see
For I am
you, through and through
But sometimes
reflection
I wish that
I resembled you.

Prologue

When he lunged at her, the key she held went straight into his eye socket. He screamed then wailed as his groin connected with her knee. She cringed at the squelching sound when she pulled the key out of his eye. As the blood flowed down his face, he sobbed and rolled around holding his groin area. She stabbed the key into the side of his neck, connecting with an artery. Blood spurted like water from a fireman's hose.

She moved a few steps from the body and dipped her toes into the water. She glanced back at him every now and again. Until he stopped moving. She went back and listened to see if he was dead: he was. Finally. She rolled him, like a sack of potatoes, deeper and deeper into the water. With every push, the corpse seemed lighter and lighter.

Archimedes was right.

When he was as far out as she could manage, she swam back to the shore and gathered her clothes and redressed.

She left his things where he'd dropped them.

As the new day's sun turned the sky a fiery red, she returned to the water.

She scanned the shoreline and saw no sign of him. She dipped the key into the water to rinse the blood off, then skipped home. After a long shower, she slept like a baby.

Chapter One

THIS IS THE STORY of a woman who was too nice for her own good: until she wasn't.

Ribby Balustrade's day always began in the same way, with her mother threatening to feed her breakfast to their Wolfhound Scamp if she didn't hurry up.

Ribby, whose wardrobe was limited to her mother's hand-me-downs pulled the flowered muumuu over her head, stepped into her Jesus sandals, and brushed her hair, which didn't take long. Still, she rarely made it down in time.

Martha Balustrade wasn't the kind of mother who stuck to a specific schedule. Breakfast would be prepared. What and when, was decided on the day.

The winner of this never-ending kitchen debacle was Scamp.

"It's fine, I'm not hungry anyway," Ribby lied, as she patted the dog on the forehead, and left the house.

Ribby didn't dwell on these, her very own Groundhog Day events. Instead, she hurried her way through the park to the main street.

The bus shelter reeked of urine and coffee. On a day like today, she was glad to have missed breakfast, for even now the stench made her retch. She couldn't wait to get to work at the library.

When the bus arrived, she flashed her Presto card, then made her way to her usual seat at the back. Her stomach rumbled, as the bus bumped along, stopping now and then to take on new passengers. Arriving in downtown Toronto, she exited the bus and hurried into the corner store for a quick chocolate bar and then on to the library.

Ribby prided herself in never being late. One simply couldn't be late if one worked in a library. If you were, you'd have hordes of impatient patrons clogging up the entryway. And so, it was, when she entered and saw the exceptionally long queue with Mr. Filchard leading the pack.

"Good morning, Mr. Filchard. How may I help you?"

"Good morning, dear Ribby. Oh, what would I do without you? Everyone else is always so busy, busy, busy—but you, you my dear, you always make time to help an old man."

"Just doing my job," Ribby said. "Now, what are you looking for today?"

"Could you please come closer? It's a rather rude book: *Tropic of Cancer*. Do you know it?"

"Yes, Mr. Filchard. It's a classic."

"Is it? I heard it has, oh never mind; if it's a classic then I don't need to whisper anymore, do I?"

"No, there are far more controversial books," she smiled remembering the hoo-ha over fifty shades of nonsense.

"Problem is, my dear, I have no idea who wrote it. You know me, I'm from the dark ages and can't use those blasted computer thingies." He laughed. "Would you be a love and look it up for me?"

"It's written by Henry Miller," she said as she clicked into the database. "Yes, it's available just upstairs in the fiction aisle."

"I'll have a look first. Henry Miller, you say. Never heard of him!"

"To tell you the truth, I wasn't that impressed when I read it. The critics and reviewers thought it was brilliant in its time. There are some rude bits."

"Thanks, Ribby. Have a nice day."

"You're very welcome," she said as he toddled off.

She managed the other waiting customers single-handedly. After she finished helping the last one, she tidied the counter.

Now that things were quiet, Ribby made herself a cup of coffee and returned to her desk. On the way back, she stopped for a moment to take in the sound of water. The library's architect, in using the fountain to mask the external noises had been inciteful. Some cities were closing their libraries, but Toronto was different. The building itself was a survivor. Even looting after the War of 1812 did not break its spirit.

She took a sip of coffee and stood for a moment, glancing at the stairs. They looked cool, with people going up and coming down, but the elevator sure came in handy when it was required.

On the stairwell above, she noticed Mr. Filchard making his way down. Nearly at the bottom, he had one hand on his book and the other on his library card. She stopped and waited for him. He was a little out of breath.

"I'll definitely take the elevator next time," Mr. Filchard said.

They made their way to the help desk where Ribby stamped his card.

"Dirty old man!" Amanda, a co-worker whispered as he left the building. "He sure gives me the creeps."

Ribby ignored her comments. She picked up an armful of books, put them onto a trolley and pushed it into the elevator and went up to the third floor. She moved from shelf to shelf filing away. While refiling a book near to the window, a flash from across the street caught her eye. A young man in his early twenties, dressed from head to toe in denim strode in her direction. Sunlight glinted on his nose rings and the chains attaching them to his ears.

Ribby continued watching as he walked up the stairs. Curious, she hurried down to the main floor.

The mere thought of serving him, made her heart race. She'd never been so close to a bloke who had so many holes in his head before. Ribby was certain others had disguised holes—emotional wounds hidden deep inside. Like Vincent Van Gogh who used his pain to express emotion. The concept of using your body as art both frightened and intrigued her.

She arrived back at the desk, watching him. He stood in the entryway like a little boy lost. *What's his voice like*, she wondered?

She positioned herself behind the Acquisition Section where she tidied up. He hadn't moved an inch. She coughed, then stood under the Help/Information sign. Their eyes met.

"May I help?" Ribby asked with flushed cheeks and sweaty palms.

"Uh, yea, well, I hope so," he said in a loud voice.

"Please speak more quietly," she said.

"Oh, Okay. Sorry. I'm looking for a book, but I don't know its name."

"Do you know who wrote it?"

"No."

"Can tell me what the book is about?"

"Yep, yep, that I do know, that I do know for sure. It's about the future. Well, when the guy wrote it, it was *his* future. To us, it's our past. It has *Big Brother* in it. Not the TV show mind you, another kind of *Big Brother*." He laughed at the clever way he'd tied both the past and the present together. Ribby laughed too.

"Oh, you mean *1984* by George Orwell?"

"Yep, that sounds right. Orwell. Excellent. Is it in?"

"One moment please," Ribby said as she typed it into the computer. It was in, and Ribby went along to find it. The young man trailed behind her.

When she had the book in hand, they returned to the front desk. Ribby confirmed he had the necessary identification and issued a library card.

Transaction complete, he popped the card into his ratty wallet. He thanked Ribby and sauntered off toward the exit. His ripped blue jeans sagged—like Ribby's state of mind.

Shift finally over, Ribby rushed out of the building. Every Monday, Ribby volunteered at the children's hospital. She danced and sang. She did anything she could to raise their spirits. She adored the children, and they seemed to return the feeling. Each week, she picked one child to be the centre of attention. Today, it was Mikey Landers' turn and she mustn't be late.

In her left hand, Ribby carried her magic bag. The children were always excited when she let them dip their hand in. Items inside included: costumes, musical instruments, face paint, balloons, trinkets, and makeup.

When she finally arrived in the children's ward, she skipped into Mikey's room. His parents were sitting, one on each side of the bed, gripping their son's hands in a pile of fingers and palms. They wiped tears away with their free hands. Mikey was asleep, so she quietly left.

Ribby tried not to think about the sadness which hung in the air in Mikey's room. Mikey and his family had been through so much.

She pushed it away, into the back of her mind. Ribby's role was to cheer up the children and their families. They'd be waiting for her. She put on her happiest face.

Billy and Janie Freeman let out a yell when they spotted Ribby coming down the hall. "She's here! She's here!" they cried. A wave of glee filled the corridor. Children and their families formed a circle around her in the Common Room.

Ribby sang a self-composed number called *Jump Like A Caribou* and played the kazoo at appropriate moments:

JUMP JUMP JUMP
LIKE A CARIBOU!

Ribby started a train and the children who could walk fell in behind her.

JUMP JUMP JUMP
LIKE A CARIBOU

The old train ended and Ribby formed a line of the children who were in wheelchairs or on crutches. The children sang or waved or stamped their feet. Any action they could to help them get into the song and make some noise.

JUMP JUMP JUMP
LIKE A CARIBOU!

When the song finished, they cried, "Again! Again!"

The song was familiar to the children as Ribby often sang it using different animals like the kangaroo, the cockatoo, the cockapoo, and she even had a version which included a visit to the zoo.

Ribby bowed and went straight into a different tune. She enjoyed mixing things up. Keeping them guessing. When the energy in the room waned, she changed courses, asking for balloon shape requests. She sang as she pulled and twisted the balloons into animal shapes. The most popular request was for a mother caribou and her calf which kept her busy as it was a difficult task.

The children who wanted balloons had them and it was time for Ribby to go. She started packing up her bag, just when Mikey Landers entered strumming the wheels of his chair. His mom trailed behind him, having trouble catching up. Mikey was cross, she could see that immediately. She went to him, offering an animal balloon with her hand outstretched.

"I, I almost missed you, Ribby! You should have woken me up. You promised to do your act from my room this week! It was my turn!" Tears fell down his cheeks as he crossed his arms and refused her peace offering.

Lowering her hand, she knelt to be at his level and said, "Sorry, sport. I'm so happy to see you up and about now," —she looked at his parents— "but you were snoozin' when I went by kiddo. I know how much you need your beauty sleep! You're top of the list for next week, okay?"

"Promise?" He uncrossed his arms.

"Cross my heart and hope to die." Ribby wished she could take those words back and swallow them. If it were possible to exchange her life for his, she would have done it there and then without hesitation.

Mikey hadn't noticed the faux-pas, and he finally reached out and accepted her gift.

After she handed it to him Ribby said goodbye. On the way out of the room, she said, "See you next week, Rugrats!"

Ribby held her tears back until she was out of the building. Having no tissues, she used her sleeve. By the time she reached the bus stop she had managed to calm herself down.

Every single week, she promised herself she wouldn't cry. Children should be out playing, having fun. They shouldn't have to worry about being sick or dying. If she could take that pain away... Even for a short period of time, then it was worth taking a ride on the emotional roller-coaster.

THE BUS WOULDN'T ARRIVE for fifteen more minutes. She rushed to the corner store in response to her grumbling stomach. *Salty or sweet?* she thought. Behind the counter she spotted an array of cigarettes. Curious, she asked for a pack.

"Which kind, lady?"

She glanced at their names. "Cools," she said.

"Have a lighter already?" the sales guy asked. Without waiting for an answer, he placed a pack of matches on top of the Cools. "The matches are on the house," he said as Ribby handed over the cash. He returned the change.

The clerk's sudden grin, which resembled a grimace, disturbed her. She hightailed it out of there. Back at the bus stop she tore open the cigarette pack and lit one. She inhaled deeply, like an actress playing a part. It looked so easy in the movies. In reality it was difficult not to throw-up. After the initial drag, she blew out the smoke and relaxation swept over her.

When the bus arrived, she popped the packet into her purse and took her usual seat at the back. She thought about how naughty it would be to smoke a cigarette on *Stan the Man's* bus.

Stan the Man was a bit of a Nazi and a renowned bully. She'd seen it herself. Yelling at kids for putting their feet on the seats. Throwing them off the bus in the freezing cold, like they'd committed murder or something.

Once, a little old lady had her bags taking up the seat beside her. He demanded she remove them even though no one needed the seat. When she wouldn't comply, he threw her off the bus.

Ribby could still remember her prune-like face looking up as the bus started to move away. The woman had raised her middle finger up as high as her little body could put it and shouted, "Fuck you!"

Ribby had been so shocked by the incident, from that day forward she always sat at the back of the bus. She could be invisible there. She could watch like a fly on the wall without drawing attention to herself. She didn't want to do anything to piss off *Stan the Man*.

Then again, Stan couldn't see everything. Like the man picking his nose and wiping it on the seat. She saw it, but Stan didn't. Ribby laughed. Stan the Man glanced back at her in the rear-view mirror. She stopped laughing. How safe was Stan's driving ability? Obsessed with his passengers, it's a wonder he didn't get into a crash.

Ribby reached into her handbag. Considered pulling out a cigarette. *Would Stan notice? Would he throw her off the bus?* It was dark, and it was too far home to walk. She closed her handbag. She focussed on the stars out the window.

At home, she pulled open the door and immediately, laughter came from the kitchen. Her mother often had gentlemen callers over. This evening was no different.

Tom Mitchell sat across the table from her mother. Ribby nodded in Tom's direction. She felt Tom's eyes undressing her. He always looked at her like that. Her mother didn't seem to mind.

"Hello, Ribby," Tom said. "Good to see you again."

Ribby turned the tap off, took a deep breath, and faced the table.

Her mother waited for a response.

As did Tom.

"Well then," Tom said as he stood up. "I'd best be going, Martha. It was mighty fine seeing you as always." He pushed his chair back and tipped his baseball cap in her direction.

Tom took a step toward Ribby. "And you too Ribby—even though you think you're too high and mighty to say hello to your mom's beau, I still like you fine."

Ribby's mother laughed, a loud and low belly laugh. "Oh Tom, our Ribby is afraid of her own shadow. Never mind. I'm sure she likes you, too." She turned to her daughter. "Ain't that right, Ribby? You always like my beaus."

Ribby gulped down the glass of water. She reached into her handbag and touched the cigarette packet.

Knowing a secret gave her a sense of power. She went into the living room.

Tom and Martha whispered in the entryway while she leafed through a magazine. She soon grew tired of scandalous headlines and picked up the TV remote and clicked through the channels. The front door slammed.

"Wish you'd be nicer to my friends," Martha said as she plunked down on the sofa. "After all, we need friends in this life, and Tom has always been good to us."

"What's for dinner, Ma?"

"I've had company all afternoon. No time for making dinner, daughter, and I'm starving," Martha licked her lips. "Absolutely, totally and completely bloody starving."

"Let's order in then," Ribby said. "We can get some Special Fried Rice, some Egg Rolls and Lemon Chicken to share."

"Yep, that would be okay with me," Martha said, snatching the television flicker out of Ribby's hand. She pointed and clicked, fast and furious.

"I'll go to Mrs. Engle's and ring."

"You do that, daughter, you do that," Martha said as she poured herself a glass of whiskey. She shot a bit of soda into it. She reached into the mini-fridge and took out the ice cube tray. She plopped in two cubes, took a sip and sighed.

When Ribby returned Martha said. "You're a good daughter, most of the time." Martha took another longer drink. "We'd be homeless without your wages to pay the mortgage and put food on the table." Martha stirred her drink with her finger. The ice cubes clinked against the glass.

Ribby fidgeted a little. This conversation always made her feel uncomfortable.

When the commercials started Martha asked, "Any sign of the food yet? The whiskey's gnawing at my belly."

"He said thirty minutes, Mom."

"Thirty minutes, well, by God, thirty minutes is too long to wait for a little rice!" Martha slammed her left fist down on the arm of the chair. Her right arm remained aloft to preserve the sanctity of her glass of whiskey.

"I can't cancel now. Sit tight and watch your program, and it'll be here before you know it."

Martha busied herself at the bar adding more whiskey and ice. Back on the couch she was resigned to waiting for her supper.

At least she didn't have to sing for it thought Ribby with a wry grin.

***

Martha flipped through the channels. Ribby waited for the delivery person in the entryway.

She reached into her handbag and pulled out a cigarette. She placed it unlit between her lips and looked at her reflection in the mirror. If her hair wasn't so neutral and her complexion so washed out, she had potential to look sophisticated. Maybe.

Startled when the doorbell rang, she almost dropped the ciggie.

Martha yelled, "Get that, Ribby!"

She shoved the cigarette into her handbag.

Bing-bong again.

"Daughter? Daughter! Are you there?"

"Yes, Mom, I'm getting the money." She opened the door.

"Good evening," the delivery guy said.

He didn't recognize her, but she knew him. The guy from the library with piercings and tattoos.

"That'll be $32.50," he said.

Ribby handed over $35.00. He looked different standing on her porch. "Keep the change," she said as she closed the door still thinking about him.

"It must be getting cold, Rib!" Martha said, yanking the bag out of her hand and heading into the kitchen.

Ribby placed her handbag back on the hook, making a mental note to take it upstairs when she went to bed. It wouldn't do for Martha to find the cigarettes.

Back in the living room they ate dinner on TV trays. A favourite gameshow *Jeopardy!* started.

Ribby and Martha had a rivalry going whenever they watched. Whoever knew the answer first, would yell it out.

"What is New York," Ribby shouted.

"What is L.A.!" Martha yelled. She was wrong.

"I told you so," Ribby said. "Everyone knows *that* Mother."

Martha reached across the table and smacked her daughter across the face. The blow was so hard that the TV tray and its contents went flying. Ribby's chair tipped over backward, and her head hit the coffee table with a *thunk*. Then hit the floor with a *thud*.

"That'll teach you," Martha said, "for showing disrespect. This is my house. Who are you to tell me whether I'm wrong or right!"

"But Ma," Ribby whispered. "He said..."

"I don't give a rat's ass what he said. Now, I'm going to bed. Make me a cup of tea—my usual—and bring it on up."

"Okay, Ma," Ribby said.

Ribby went to the bar area. She picked up the bottle, went into the kitchen and set the kettle to boil. She plopped a teabag into a cup and poured the hot water in a quarter of the way. After the tea steeped, she added half a cup of Bourbon, followed by two teaspoons of sugar.

On her way up the stairs, she decided to do something rather un-Ribby-like.

She moved her tongue around inside her mouth, gathering saliva and letting it splosh in her cheeks. When she had enough, she spat into her mother's cup.

She watched it on the surface, then gave it a stir before setting it down on the night table. She smiled as she pulled down the top sheet, then the blankets like she did every single night.

Martha came out of the bathroom. "You're a good daughter some of the time."

Ribby said nothing. She helped her mother out of her clothes and into her nightgown. Her mother's feet were cold. Ribby massaged them with some oil before sliding her slippers over her aged flesh.

On her way out, Ribby glanced back over her shoulder. Martha took a sip of doctored tea, then sighed.

Ribby held back laughter until she was in her room.

Then she laughed so hard, she had to muffle the sound with her pillow.

Chapter Two

When she awoke, Ribby sat up and thought about the night before. She laughed, listening to her mother below stomping around as was her usual routine.

"Breakfast will be ready in ten minutes," Martha called.

Ribby managed to block out most of it. Same old. Same old.

"I'm not hungry, Ma," Ribby shouted, brushing her hair. "Besides, I have to get to work early today."

Ribby listened as her mother cursed her out. She ran a brush through her hair stopping suddenly when a cackle rang out downstairs. This laughter was disturbing. Martha rarely laughed in the morning unless one of her beaus was over.

"See ya, Ma!" Ribby said as she rounded the kitchen and made her way straight for the door. Once outside, she noticed a van with a man in it sitting and waiting. On the side of the truck the business name read: *Attics-R-Us*.

The word attic triggered a memory of the last time she'd gone up there. The mere thought of it made her shiver and shake. She neutralized the memory, locking it away with a key in the library of her imagination.

She pointed herself in the direction of the bus stop. She made it just in time. She climbed on board and stared out the window as the world passed her by in a blur. Her stomach rumbled. She grew more and more hungry. She ignored the pangs, wanting to save every penny for the trip to the mall. Today was the day she was going to treat herself.

She opened her handbag. Just smelling the tobacco deadened her tummy rumblings.

At work, she hung up her coat and secured her handbag.

Although her co-workers were at their stations, no one was helping the queue of waiting patrons.

Ribby was the most senior librarian's assistant and yet she had no authority.

Again, Ribby attended to the waiting patrons single-handedly. Head Librarian Mrs. P. Wilkinson did not seem to notice.

During lunch break, Ribby asked her co-workers where they bought their clothes. Most recommended the mall department store for quality brand names at affordable prices.

Ribby grew more and more excited now that she knew where she was shopping. She couldn't wait do something she had never done before.

Ribby Balustrade was going to buy herself a new dress.

***

AT THE DEPARTMENT STORE, Ribby stood for a moment outside and peered in the windows. Cars, buses, and tram noises echoed around the buildings. A busker near to the entry way began strumming and vocalising. A crowd began to gather, pushing and shoving, some carrying hot beverages and smoking cigarettes. It was so noisy and so crowded all she wanted to do was get inside. Inside into the quiet.

She entered the revolving doors and for a second, it was quiet. Then her compartment sucked open, and she stepped out into a different kind of chaos. Customers wielding bags, coming, and going. And it was big, many floors. Multiple people filled escalators going up and down. Smells of fried food, popcorn and donuts sweetened the air causing a sensory overload.

"May I help you?" a lady at the Information Desk inquired.

"Yes, Women's Wear, please."

"Third floor," she said.

It was quiet on the escalator. Travellers were looking at their phones. She held on to the bannister.

When she arrived on the third floor, she spotted it—the dress of her dreams. A little black number, as the magazines at the library would call it, perfect for evening cocktail parties and special events. She looked at it, thinking about the words from a baseball related movie. She smiled, changing the words to, "If you buy it, occasions to wear it will come."

"May I help you?" a woman in a smart suit asked.

"Yes, yes you can. I'm looking to treat myself. I thought a black dress, something easy to wear and care for would fit the bill. I love the one on the mannequin up there. If you have it in my size, I'd like to try it on."

"Excellent choice," the woman said. "Now, let me see, what size are you? Twelve? Fourteen?"

"I, I don't know."

"You're a twelve. I'm usually fairly good at guessing, but in case, take a ten, twelve and fourteen," the clerk suggested. "Oh, and you'll need a pair of black shoes, to finish off the look. Are you a Size seven?"

Surprised, Ribby said, "These shoes are Size seven."

"Perfect then. Don't be afraid to come on out when you're ready. I know how difficult it can be when you're shopping on your own."

"I, I will, thank you," Ribby said as she closed the dressing room door.

Surrounded by mirrors, Ribby could see herself from all angles for the very first time as the drab Martha hand-me-down fell to the floor.

Ribby tried on the Size twelve dress. With its neckline and pleats at the hips and waist it really accentuated her figure. She already knew she wanted to buy it, still she wanted to get a second opinion. She stepped out of the change room.

"Wow!" the clerk exclaimed. "You look amazing! But here, let me do one thing."

The clerk disappeared around the corner but returned in seconds. "Let me put this in your hair, and these faux pearls around your neck. I swear, you'll look like a million dollars!"

"I look so glam!" Ribby hardly recognized herself.

"You do look sensational!"

"I'd like to try on a couple more outfits." She walked over to a rack, picked out a two-piece red suit, a blouse, and a pair of pants. She returned to the changeroom. The suit looked wonderful, with its clean-cut jacket and matching skirt and the shoes she tried on with the dress went with it perfectly. The blouse looked better off than on and the pants drew too much attention to her butt.

"I'll take the suit, the dress, the shoes and the pearls," Ribby said. "How much is it? I forgot to look."

The clerk added everything up. "Total cost before tax is $760.00. Will that be cash or credit?"

"Oh, that's more than I expected," Ribby confessed.

"Not to worry, why don't you take the dress today and then, come back later for the shoes and accessories. Or you can apply for In-Store Credit. I'll verify you qualify and then you can get instant credit."

"Could I?" Ribby asked. "That would be helpful!"

The clerk asked Ribby a few questions and she qualified for a credit card. She bought the lot. The clerk bagged everything up.

"Thank you so much. You've been wonderful!"

"You're very welcome."

Ribby celebrated with a cup of coffee and as it was getting dark, made her way to the bus stop. On the way, she smoked a cigarette.

The *Attics-R-Us* van was still parked outside her house when she rounded the corner.

Once inside, Ribby went into the kitchen. Behind the closed door, familiar sounds of lovemaking reached her ears. It wasn't the first time she'd returned home, to find her mother with one of her beaus. The Attics-R-Us guy here all day? Ewwww. Ribby retreated upstairs.

In her room, Ribby compartmentalized the downstairs incident. She wouldn't let it spoil her day.

She put on her new dress, shoes, and pearl necklace. She reached into her handbag and pulled out a cigarette. With it in her hand she looked even more sophisticated. She played with her hair. Testing how it looked up and then down.

Outside, a vehicle door opened then closed. Ribby peered out the window and watched as the Attics-R-Us van pulled away.

Moments later her mother's footsteps sounded, and in the other room the shower started up.

Ribby changed back into her old clothes. As she undressed, she pushed the thoughts of her mother and her beaus out of her mind. When she was ready, she quietly tiptoed downstairs, out the door and came back in again. This action strengthened her compartmentalizing for this incident, and it would help her in the future when a similar incident occurred. With Martha's array of gentlemen callers, this action was a self preservation tactic.

She poured herself a cup of hot tea and gave the stew in the crockpot a stir, before going into the living room to watch a bit of tv.

Martha came downstairs shortly there-after and they ate dinner. Once her mother fell asleep on the couch, Ribby went upstairs to her room.

After reading for awhile, Ribby closed her eyes and let her imagination run. She envisioned a home of her own, on the waterfront. She imagined the living room with a comfy love seat and matching crunchy chairs. On the wall behind them Van Gogh and Monet prints. Flowers in vases. She imagined coming home from work, putting her feet up. Having control of the television.

The bubble burst and reality seeped in.

Martha would never allow it.

What she didn't know, couldn't hurt her though.

In addition to the newly acquired credit card, Ribby participated in the Provincial Library Staff Savings Program, so she had some secret savings but hadn't touched them until today.

Ribby thought about an article she'd read in the newspaper. It was the true story of a man who had two different lives with two different wives. She wondered if she could take the idea and make it her own. Could she create a new life for herself?

Sleep came, but Ribby didn't dream. Instead, she decided.

For tomorrow, she would give birth to a new version of herself. An imaginary friend. An alter-ego.

A part of herself, who would do things she was too afraid to do.

A friend with a beautiful name: *Angela.*

Chapter Three

SATURDAY MORNING. RIBBY JUMPED out of bed excited about the day ahead. She folded her black dress, some tights and put them into her handbag. Her heels wouldn't fit. A pair of sandals would have to do.

Martha sat at the kitchen table with her head in her hands. Hangover mode. The coffee percolator snuffled and hissed behind her. When she saw Ribby, she moaned. Ribby had seen the signs of too much whiskey in her mother many times before. She poured herself a cup of coffee and refilled her mother's cup. Martha's hands shook when she took a sip.

Ribby continued down the hall and out onto the front porch where she picked up the newspaper. She returned to the kitchen and sipped on her now cool coffee while she read. The paper proved to be no barrier for Martha's slurps interspersed with moans.

Ribby flipped ahead to the Apartments For Rent column. She ran her finger down the list and there were plenty to choose from in the waterfront area she hoped to live in. She closed the paper and rinsed out her cup.

"I have to run, Ma. See you later."

Martha slammed her fists on the table. "Don't come back then, if you can't even muster up an ounce of sympathy for your poor ol' Ma."

"Take a couple Tylenols and you'll be fine," Ribby said as she opened the front door and slammed it behind her. As she walked away, she noticed her mother had closed the front blinds. No gentlemen callers today.

Ribby caught the bus and after arriving in the prime rental area, she purchased another newspaper. She circled a couple of possibilities and decided to attend some Open House viewings. One was in a splendid area not far from the beach and was number one on her priority list.

Before she could view the properties, she needed to change into a suitable outfit. A public washroom would do. Dressed in her new gear, she explored the area, taking time to look at Lake Ontario. She listened while the gentle waves sloshed upon the shores. Above her the seagulls cried out for attention. Behind her cars honked as passengers waited for the lights to change. The sound of AC-DC with strong bass rang out and she turned to see a black car with the top down was the culprit. She continued along the promenade. Her mouth watered when she came upon a hotdog stand with onions frying on the side. She checked out the time in a shop window and realised she had to hurry to view the first house.

From the outside, the building looked inviting. It wasn't a skyscraper like some of the others. It was mid-size with private balconies. Balconies adorned with personal belongings such as bikes and plants. Balconies where tenants created their own little bit of heaven. Where they took pride in their properties.

    She spotted a *For Rent* sign above her. As promised in the advertisement it had a water-front-view. She couldn't wait to get up there and take a closer look.

    Once inside, she meandered around the lobby getting a feel for the place. In the mail area she read the names adorning boxes, almost like she hoped to recognize someone. She didn't. She pushed the button for the elevator and made her way up.

    It was easy to find the apartment with signage pointing the way. The door was open. She knocked anyway, then went inside. Others were milling around. On first impression she knew she had to get the apartment. It was meant for her.

    The agent in the kitchen spoke to a young couple. To her he said, "I'll be with you in a moment. Feel free to have a look around."

    The interior was a bland shade of magnolia. The kitchen was well-equipped with stainless steel appliances including a dishwasher. The main living area was open plan. Perfect. She imagined sitting there, looking out at the amazing view of the waves. Listening to the waves. She slid open the balcony doors and stepped out. Children played not far away. She went back inside and viewed the bedroom. It was bigger than her room at home, had an en-suite and a more than ample walk-in closet. She'd have to buy a lot of new shoes and clothes to fill that space. It was wonderful. Everything. She wanted it so bad she could taste it.

"The view is breathtaking," Ribby said when the agent was free. "This is exactly what I'm looking for."

"It's in demand. If you want it," the agent said. "You'll need to fill out an application today. Have you ever rented before?"

"No, I've been living at home."

He fiddled with some papers. "Will you be living alone? Do you work fulltime?"

"Yes, and yes. I work at the Library. I'm Assistant Librarian, and I've been working there for seven years."

"The owner prefers to rent to a single person or a young couple...if everything checks out with the paperwork."

Ribby's eyes lit up as she accepted the application. The agent offered her a pen. As she filled it in, he chatted away.

"Once your application gets accepted, we'll need a cheque to cover first and last month's rent."

"No problem." She finished the form with a signature. "When will I know if my application is successful?"

"I'll give you a call. We should know by Tuesday."

"I, we don't have a phone. If you give me your business card, I'll ring you. Is Tuesday morning, okay?"

"Perfect," he glanced at the application. "Uh, Ms. Balustrade, talk to you then, and good luck," the agent said as he removed the Open House sign. He walked her to the elevator and out of the building. When they reached the street he asked, "Can I give you a lift anywhere?"

"No, thank you, I'm going to take a walk along waterfront, then catch a bus home."

Ribby ran to the beach. She slipped off her sandals and let the sand ooze out between her toes. Then she dipped them into the water. She collected a few shells, sat down, and listened to the sounds of the city and of Lake Ontario.

A seagull landed nearby. Then another.

"What do you think?" she asked the birds. "Is this the place for Angela and I?"

The seagulls looked at her, but a squawk was their only reply.

***

IT WAS STILL EARLY—TOO early to go home. Ribby decided to go check out some furniture. In the showroom, there had been a good selection of items. It was all so expensive though since she needed everything.

A voice in her head said, *Second hand. Elegance. Sophistication. Shabby chic.*

Ribby looked around. Had someone spoken to her? She was alone. She ran her fingers along the back of a sofa thinking, Shabby chic huh? Perfect.

The voice said, *Don't forget—a new apartment requires a new wardrobe.*

Ribby paused. Was she going crazy? She was having a conversation with herself, but the voice was different. The voice was Angela. Angela had been born.

You can't expect me to be born into this life wearing Martha's old rags.

Ribby smiled. Agreed. First things first though. Apartment. Furniture. You need beautiful things. We need beautiful things. We'll have to make sure Mom never finds out. She'd have a cow.

She is a cow.

Ribby laughed until she almost wet her pants.

How did I ever get along without you?

We'll never know. Hey, are you ever going to light up a ciggie? My lungs are crying out for one!

Ribby reached in her handbag and pulled out a cigarette. She slipped it between her lips, lit the end and took a drag.

Ahhhhh, Angela sighed, *I needed that. Ribby, now, we need a plan.*

I know. If we get this apartment, how are we going to keep it from Mother? How am I going to continue paying her and pay for the new place, plus get everything else? I know, I'll ask for a raise.

Don't ask for a raise, demand one. And get the old bag to reduce your rent!

I'm overdue for a raise. You're right about that. But, as for Mom, she'll never agree even though she'd lose the house without me.

That's her problem, not yours Rib. She's a grown woman and if you're not around, she'll be able to rent out your room, right?

It felt strange to Ribby, to have someone on her side for once.

I don't intend to stay at the apartment fulltime. That would never do. She'd find a way of spoiling everything. No, I'll live at home during the week and at the apartment on weekends.

She'll go through your bankbook though, again, Rib and she'll see the balance going down, down and she'll hit the roof. You know what she's like.

Ribby did a double take. How did Angela know about that?

You're right; I'll have to be careful about where I leave my purse. With the ciggies in it, I've been taking it straight up to my room. I'll continue doing so, and she'll be none the wiser.

And if she asks you for money, what are you going to do?

I'm going to tell her no.

Remember the time you offered to hand over every cent you made? All she had to do, was stop accepting gentlemen callers?

And how does she know about that? It's like she's been with me all the time.

Yes, how could I ever forget? Mother laughed so hard, I thought she was choking. I tried to help her get air, by hitting her on the back, and in return she hit me so hard my tooth fell out.

The old cow will miss you, Ribby, but you deserve a life, and I'm here to help you. To see that you get one. Now, we better get back before the old mare sends out the cavalry!

Happiness was within sight, but sometimes you had to reach out and take it.

Chapter Four

MONDAY MORNING, RIBBY WAS up and out the door very early. She didn't want to see Martha. For work, she wore a Martha-muumuu specialty in which her breasts fought frontal frills. This attire was within the library's wardrobe policy. She hurried to catch the bus and arrived earlier than usual.

"Good morning, Ribby," Mrs. Pigeon a regular library goer said. "If you're looking for something excellent to read, I recommend this one." She held the book out and Ribby took it.

"*My Life on a Plate*," Ribby read. "Is it about food?"

"No, not in any way or form!" Mrs. Pigeon said laughing. "It's about life, laughter and tears." She paused. "Stop that, Billy! Jason, get back here." The children returned to the counter. "I'm sorry the book is a late return."

"You've sold me on it. Thanks, Mrs. Pigeon." She smiled as she stamped the book returned.

"You're very welcome, dear. Next time I come in you can tell me what you thought of Clare Hutt. Say bye-bye to Ribby now, boys. Jason stop spitting at your brother. You're going to be in so much trouble when you get home!" Mrs. Pigeon smiled as she led Jason by the ear and Billy by the hand. The trio exited through the revolving doors.

Ribby was too excited to read. Besides, it was Monday again and she had to get to the hospital.

At 5 p.m., Ribby grabbed her things from her locker and caught the bus. En-route she felt tempted to smoke, but she didn't want the children to smell cigarettes on her.

She went to the gift shop where she had requested helium filled balloons for every child in the ward. The thought was wonderful, carrying them was another matter.

As promised, Ribby started at Mikey Landers' room. He was not there. She proceeded along the corridor, popping her head into rooms along the way. Behind her others followed forming a singing parade. Wheelchairs, crutches, everyone was welcome. Even Head Nurse Alice joined in.

Ribby glanced in her direction and their eyes met. Something was wrong, but it could wait. She continued with the performance.

Ribby stepped into the centre. She made eye contact with the children. Lucy May Monroe needed a ribbon for her hair, which Ribby pulled out of her magic bag. It was a purple ribbon, Lucy May's favourite colour. The child squealed with delight. Lucy's mother wrapped it around her stubby little ponytail.

Last visit Benjamin Fish had wished for a Dragon stuffy, which Ribby now had hidden in her magic bag. She let Benjamin reach in, and he pulled it out. He put it onto his lap—looking for his parents but they weren't around. Not wanting to open it up without them, he cradled the gift in his wheel-chaired lap.

There were several other children waiting. One by one Ribby fulfilled their wishes. She sang again. This time she danced and performed her rendition of Elton John's *Crocodile Rock*. She handed out the rest of the balloons. Only Mikey Landers' balloon remained.

Ribby said good-bye to the children. She carried Mikey's red balloon and walked along the corridor. Nurse Alice was waiting.

"Ribby, wait, I have something to tell you."

Ribby didn't want to hear the news. She continued walking. If she didn't know, then it wouldn't be true.

Nurse Alice caught Ribby's arm. "Ribby, Mikey was in a lot of pain and now he's at peace."

Ribby wanted to scream. She continued walking and left the building. Once outside, she let the balloon go, then watched until she could see it nor more.

She did not cry.

Chapter Five

RIBBY WAS SO EXCITED when she called the estate agent from a pay phone and found out the apartment was hers. In a little over a week, she'd be moving in. Plenty of time to buy some necessities and figure out how she was going to stay away from Martha.

Why not use me? After all, we are friends, aren't we?
What do you mean?
Sometimes you're as thick as a brick. Tell the old battle-axe you're visiting a friend who lives in the city, and her name is Angela.
What if she wants to meet you? Plus, I can't lie; my complexion would give me away.
You're not telling a lie. You will be spending the time with me. You have the perfect alibi— ME!

That night at dinner, Ribby broached the subject. "I'd like to go out on Friday night with my friend, Angela."

"Do tell?!" Martha said with astonishment in her voice. "You have a friend?"

"We read the same books and we get along."

"Daughter do be careful of this new friend. Watch she doesn't take advantage because you're very naïve about worldly things."

"I'll be fine, Mom. We're seeing a movie and getting a cup of coffee."

The days went by more quickly now that her life was out of its usual rut and soon it was Friday.

"I better get moving. We're meeting outside the theatre."

"Before you go could you give your poor old mom a few dollars to replace the bottle of Jack Daniels?"

Ribby hesitated. If she didn't give her mother money, she might not get out of the house. She had to hand over the cash, and so she did.

"I'll be late, Mom; no sense waiting up for me."

"Have a good time," Martha said stuffing the cash into her bra.

Walking along the pathway, Ribby took in several deep breaths. She couldn't believe it. Friday night and she was going out on the town to the movies.

Don't forget about me.

How could I? Without you, I'd still be standing there in the front room!

You did good Ribby, in giving her the money tonight. But no more. We'll need every Loonie!

During the movie, Angela kept giggling at the lovey dovey bits.

This is so boring! Talk about unrealistic. Let's get out of here.

It's romantic. Give it a chance.

Ribby stuffed a piece of chocolate into her mouth.

Wish we could smoke in here.

Shhhh.

After the movie, Ribby felt too annoyed to get a coffee and headed home.

What are you going say when we get back if you-know-who is up?

She won't be up. After the Jack Daniels, she'll be out for the count.

Then in the morning, you can tell her you're staying at your new friend Angela's house on Saturday night. You'll be back on Sunday evening. Got it?

She'd know I was lying. She always knows.

Maybe she will, but that was before getting your own place. A double life. Before you had me. Besides, it's a technicality. You ARE staying at my house and I am your friend. So... you really are telling the truth.

When you put it that way, it sounds rather good.

Yeah, now light up a cigarette and let's make our way back.

Chapter Six

It was move in day and Ribby was ready to go. She tiptoed down the stairs hoping to sneak away unnoticed. It was short-lived as Martha was waiting for her in the kitchen.

"Cup of coffee?"

"Thanks, Ma," Ribby said as she sat down and glanced at her watch.

Martha's gulping and the refrigerator buzzing were the only sounds heard.

"Angela and I had an incredibly good time last Friday night, Mom, and she's asked me to stay at her place for the weekend. I'd like to go."

Martha poked her nose into her cuppa. She fingered the tablecloth with one hand while petting Scamp under the table with the other.

Her mother's silence was unsettling. She'd rarely been so quiet. Ribby felt guilty and her hands trembled as she sipped her drink. She wondered if her mother knew.

Ribby thought about saying something, the silence was awful, but she was afraid to. She finished her coffee, stood up, and rinsed out the cup. She placed it into the rack to dry.

"I'm glad you have a friend and I hope you enjoy yourself."

"Thanks, Ma," Ribby said as she ran upstairs to get her handbag and went out. She caught the bus and made it clear across town before the delivery guys did.

"Come on up!" she said, speaking into the intercom. The men carted in the modest furniture and other items she'd accumulated during her lunch hours. After they left, she made herself at home, listening to the waves from the balcony.

At noon, Ribby took a stroll along the waterfront. She noticed several bars and nightclubs along the way. She'd never been in one before because going alone didn't seem interesting, but now it was different. She'd return later.

With Angela in the world, she didn't feel quite so alone.

***

Later that evening, Ribby waited on the sidewalk in front of the night club.

Stop that pacing, Ribby. I'm going to count to ten and then we're going in. All right let's go! Ready or not, here we come!

I'm frightened.

Piece of cake, Ribby, piece of cake! Follow me.

Like I have any choice in the matter.

The stairs were narrow and dimly lit. Ribby's ankles wobbled in her new high-heeled shoes as she made her way down. When she turned the corner into the bar area, the strobe lights flashed and pulsed in tune with the music.

Stop fussing about the shoes. Paradise awaits! Over here. I'm going to plant myself on this stool—so I can check out the action. Not to mention, they can check us out!

I don't know. Won't we look desperate?

Not desperate—available. Look at this place Rib. It's full of laughter, music; we'll have a fantastic time. Now, why don't you buy us a drink?

What should I ask for? I've never ordered a drink before.

Let's see, Angela perused the drinks menu. *One of these would be good. Yes, order a Vodka and Tonic—make it a large one!*

Ribby cleared her throat, hoping to attract the attention of the bartender. He was having a conversation with a man at the other end of the strip. She coughed, but with the loud music and the strobing lights, she didn't think she'd ever get noticed.

Do I have to do **everything**? Angela moaned. "Excuse me Mr. Bartender; can I get a large V&T over here when you have a sec, please?"

The bartender looked over at Ribby, and he smiled. "Sure thing."

He made his way along the bar, glancing in Ribby's direction as he mixed the drink. "You don't look familiar. Are you from around here?"

"I moved in this weekend. Thought I'd check out the action," Angela said.

"Welcome to the neighbourhood. And this is on the house. I'm the welcoming committee," the bartender said with a wink.

Angela batted Ribby's eyelids at him. She leaned over, like she meant to whisper something in his ear. Her breasts fell forwards in the dress, giving the bartender a full view of Ribby's cleavage. "Thank you very much," Angela said. "I've always wanted to meet the welcoming committee."

"Now you have, in the flesh. My name's Jake, what's yours?"

"I'm Angela, pleased to meet you."

"If you need anything else, just whistle. You know how to whistle, don't you?"

"Like the great actress Lauren Bacall once said, you just put your lips together and blow." Jake laughed, and Angela let out a faint whistle.

This comment surprised Ribby since she'd never mastered the art of whistling. Not to mention she'd never seen any of Lauren Bacall's films.

Jake moved along the bar and served another customer who'd been watching the exchange.

"Jake, old man," the man said moving in closer. "How about a beer over here?"

"Nigel. Dude. Haven't seen you in weeks. How the hell are you? I thought you moved away?"

"Me? Move? Where else could you possibly move after living near the beach for most of your life? Nowhere else compares! They'd have to take me out in a wooden box," Nigel said, laughing as Jake poured the beer.

"What have you been up to?"

"Work, work, work, enough said," Nigel said. Beckoning Jake closer, he whispered, "Who's the babe? Are you going out with her or can I have a go?"

"She's new. Moved here today. Name's Angela. Great set of knockers and not a bad sense of humour either."

See, he likes us!

He doesn't even know us.

But he wants to.

"Excuse me, Jake," Angela said. "I'd like to order a large Martini, shaken not stirred. Make that a double."

"One double Martini, coming up," Jake said.

"So, you're a James Bond fan, are you?" Jake asked as he placed the Martini in front of her.

Angela played with the olive swirling it around in the glass and then knocked the whole thing back.

Ribby shivered. As before, she'd never seen a single James Bond film, nor had she read any of Ian Flemings' novels. She wondered how Angela could know things she didn't know.

Angela was talking. "Sean Connery's portrayal was my favourite Bond. They should've stopped making the films after he quit." She pushed her glass across the bar, "Another double Martini for me please, Jake."

"Whoa, that's pretty strong stuff," Jake paused. "Are you sure you're up to another double, so soon?"

"I'm the customer, aren't I, and you're the welcoming committee, so make me feel welcome. I promise I'll be good," Angela said.

Jake looked down the bar at Nigel sitting on his own. Ten guys came walking down the stairs, ogling Ribby. "I'd like to introduce you to a friend of mine. Nigel, this is Angela. She might appreciate a little company. Nigel knows the area well, and he's a good guy. I can vouch for him."

"Very nice to meet you," Nigel said, as he extended his hand.

"Nice to meet you, too," Angela said, as she moved to avoid numb bum. She swished around the olive in the fresh Martini and stabbed it. She popped it into her mouth and poured the second drink down her gullet.

"I hear you're new in the area?" Nigel said, as he watched a tiny bit of martini seeping out of the corner of Angela's mouth.

Ribby picked up a napkin and patted the liquid away. It still tasted awful. Like she imagined nail polish remover would taste. How could Angela enjoy something which she herself did not enjoy?

"Yes, we rented an apartment. It's beautiful here," Angela said.

"We?"

Ribby cringed.

Angela laughed. "We as in the royal sense. I live by myself."

"Would you like to dance?" Nigel asked.

Ribby had never danced in her life.

Angela attempted to get down from the stool. She lost her balance and stumbled.

Nigel grabbed hold of her arm. "Whoa, are you okay?"

"I'm fine," Angela said. "Or I will be once I go to the little girl's room. Any idea where it is?"

"It's right there, at the end of the bar."

"Okie dokie," Angela said. She grabbed Nigel by the collar and looked into his deep blue eyes. "Don't you move. I'll be back in a few secs and will take you up on that offer for a dance."

Ribby took a deep breath as Nigel nodded and backed away.

Angela patted down her dress.

Once in the stall, Ribby leaned against the metal door which felt cool on her back. She tore off reams of toilet paper and covered the seat before she sat down.

The room was spinning.

Think I'm going to be sick.

Nah, we're not going to be sick, Rib. We're going to sit here for another second or two. Then we're going to go out to the sink and splash some water onto our face. We'll be fine. I promise.

A few moments later, Angela sauntered her way up to Nigel. He looked concerned. He wasn't good-looking, but he wasn't ugly either. He was kind of normal looking. He wore black jeans, a light blue t-shirt, and black boots. She liked his little beard.

"Come on, then," Angela said, taking Nigel's hand into hers and leading him onto the dance floor.

It was a slow song.

Ribby didn't even know how to be held. Her palms dripped with perspiration.

Nigel held her at arm's length.

"Closer," Angela whispered, pulling him in by cupping his buttocks.

As Chris de Burgh crooned *Lady in Red*, Angela laid her head upon Nigel's shoulder and relaxed. Ribby relaxed too. She could feel his heart beating against hers. She could feel his breath on her neck.

Angela wanted to take him home.

Ribby did not.

***

After the dance, Angela grabbed Nigel's hand and pulled him back toward the bar. They sat on the stools, knees touching. Nigel flashed two fingers in the bartender's direction and said, "Tequila."

Angela pushed her hair behind her ear and leaned in close, "Are you trying to get me drunk?"

"Uh, no. That's not my style."

Angela touched his knee when the drinks arrived.

Nigel threw back his shot. "Uh, so, what do you do? I mean for a living. I mean, I think we're moving along a little bit fast here."

I agree!

Shhh Ribby. Go back to sleep. Then to Nigel, "A little of this and a little of that." She tossed back the shot of tequila and put the lime between her teeth.

"Ah, a woman of mystery, eh?" He laughed. "Well, I'm in Public Relations."

"How exciting! Have you always worked for the same company?"

"Yes. One of the top ten companies recruited me straight from Uni. When you start off working for the best, the only way to go is down."

"I hear you. So, what do you like to do? That is, besides P.R. and hanging out in bars."

"I don't usually hang out in bars."

"Sure, sure," Angela said.

"Honestly," Nigel said, brushing her knee with his hand.

Ribby felt anxious. He was getting too familiar. She wanted to leave.

Angela liked it.

Nigel continued, "I know Jake. We've known each other for years, so I come here to the Cat's Eye once in awhile, to get out. You can't stay in your apartment watching Netflix or playing Xbox games all the time. It's better to get out. To meet people, and this area is such a happening place!"

"It is, but right now I'd murder a cup of coffee. Would you like to go somewhere else, less noisy and buy a girl a cuppa? I'd ask you back to mine, but it's a total mess since I only moved in today," Ribby said.

I told you to leave this to me. Butt out.

"There's a little café not too far away, and then I'll walk you home. If that's okay with you, Angela?"

One cup of coffee, I'm fine with that.

Take a chill pill.

Ribby and Nigel walked arm in arm to the Night Owl Café where they ordered cappuccinos. They chatted informally until 1 a.m., when Ribby said she wanted to go home.

"You're such a gentleman for asking to escort me home. I'm glad Jake introduced us."

When they arrived at Ribby's place Nigel asked, "Can I get your phone number? I'd like to see you again."

"No phone yet," Angela said as she rummaged in her purse for the keys. When she looked back up, Nigel lunged for a kiss. When his lips met Angela's, she kissed him back. Her hands ran over his shoulders and chest. His, in turn, explored.

When Ribby's knees began to buckle, she took over. Too out of breath to speak, she pulled away. "I better go in." She touched her lips. They were still tingling.

"I hope I wasn't too forward. You seemed to like it."

"I did," Angela said.

"I have to go," Ribby said. "It's been a long day, what with moving and all." She opened the door and went inside.

Nigel followed her to the open elevator. "When will I see you again?"

As the elevator began to close, Angela took over. "Next Saturday, same Bat Time, same Bat Channel."

When the doors closed, Ribby touched her lips again. It had been her first kiss and she liked it a lot.

Angela wanted more. His kiss made her hot, feverish.

She threw open the doors to the balcony. Nigel was standing there below, looking up. He waved.

"Good night, Nigel," Ribby said.

"Good night, Angela," Nigel said.

We could have invited him up you know.

I only just met him, and I don't know a thing about him. Besides, my head and my stomach feel funny.

He's perfectly harmless.

If that's true, then he'll be back.

Ribby returned inside. She closed and locked the balcony doors. She went to her en-suite and stared at herself in the mirror for quite some time, expecting to see Angela there. She could find no trace of her.

After a hot shower, Ribby fell into bed. She'd closed her bedroom door, like at home. Then it hit her, she didn't need to do that anymore. She got up, opened it wide, and then plopped back into bed. She wore her flannel nightgown because the night air had given her a chill. Once she fell back onto the pillow, the room began to spin. The ceiling was the floor, and the floor was the ceiling. When she closed her eyes, her stomach rose toward her throat. She held onto the edges of the bed like she was adrift on a lifeboat, until she could stand the spinning no more. She ran into the bathroom and vomited. Ribby made friends with that piece of porcelain, kneeling to it like it was a god.

When her stomach was empty, she stumbled back to bed and tried to sleep. The room was no longer spinning. She didn't feel comfortable with the voice inside her head. Angela seemed to know things. To have experienced things. Different than she had experienced herself. How was it possible? Why had she ordered all those Martinis?

The thought of drinking Martinis and Tequila made Ribby's stomach lunge. It was the dry heaves this time; she had nothing left to offer to the porcelain god.

She slept at the god's feet pressing her forehead to the cool porcelain.

Chapter Seven

RIBBY OPENED HER EYES. She was in the bathroom, on the floor. She lifted herself up, using the toilet bowl as an anchor. Unsteady, she put the lid down and sat on it. She turned on the tap in the sink beside her, let the water run for a few seconds, then filled a glass and took a sip. Her hands shook, as the water trickled down into her stomach.

When Ribby could stand, she held onto the sink, looked at her reflection in the mirror and vowed never drink alcohol again.

What a lightweight.

Ribby showered, dressed, and went out for a walk to clear her head. She stopped in a café and ordered a strong cup of coffee. As she sat sipping, she decided she was ready to go home, and she went and caught the bus.

That is, to Martha's home.

Did yesterday really happen? It was like a dream.

The throwing up part was more like a nightmare!

Nigel's kiss was dreamy.

My first kiss was better than pancakes with butter and syrup.

Shh, you're making me hungry.

Ribby stepped off the bus and made her way home When she turned the corner, there sat Martha, in her nightgown at 4 in the afternoon swigging from a bottle of beer.

"How's my daughter then?" Martha asked.

"We had a great time, Ma. Angela is heaps of fun. She invited me to stay again next weekend."

"Good. Everyone says you are way too serious. You need a friend your age to have some fun with."

"Who's everyone, Ma?"

Martha stood. She stumbled a bit, as Ribby backed away. The waft of beer combined with unwashed body prompted her to take shallow breaths.

"Doesn't matter. I think you need a man's company too."

"I did meet one last night named Nigel. He walked me back to Angela's place and..."

"You're away from home one night, and you get a man to walk you home! Sounds like you're more my girl than I thought you were!"

"Nothing happened."

"Not this time, daughter, but it's my blood running through those veins of yours, and time will prove what I say to be true. Once you get your hands on a man, once he starts touching you in places, oh the places, then you'll come alive. He'll take you where you never imagined your body could go. Any man can do that for you, daughter, whether you love him or not. Any man can. Any man who knows can teach you."

"I don't want to hear this," Ribby said, rushing up the stairs into her room. She slammed the door and locked it. She ran the bath, adding plenty of bubbles and selected a book from her side table. She soaked for hours, trying not to think about what Nigel might be able to teach her.

Chapter Eight

Monday morning, back at work. The usual queue of customers. Ribby serving them, Head Librarian not taking notice. Later, Ribby was on the second floor returning books to the shelves. She glanced out the window to see if anything interesting was going on, but there wasn't. Until there was. A stretch limousine across the street. A chauffeur wearing a cap got out and opened the door. Ribby watched as a pair of long legs in remarkably high-high heels attached to a blond woman got out. The chauffeur shut the door and the woman walked away in the opposite direction of the library.

I'd like to look different.

Me, too. What did you have in mind?

Our hair, we could change it. Dye it. Blonds have more fun.

Perhaps a wig instead? Less permanent.

Sounds like a plan. I can't wait!

When the books were back in their places, Ribby returned to her desk. She looked for a wig shop nearby. Wigs-R-Us was several blocks away. She glanced at the clock and it was nearly time for lunch. She could easily make it there and back. Outside the store, she looked at the wigs on display in the window.

I like that one. And that one.
Really? You'd like to go that short?
Yes, definitely shorter.
The bell rang when she entered the shop. It was noticeably quiet, quieter than the library.

"Hello?" Ribby said.

A woman popped up from behind the counter with her hand extended, "Welcome to my shop. What can I help you with today?" Even standing, she was much shorter than Ribby.

Ribby opened her mouth to speak but before she said anything the woman spoke again.

"If you'd like to sit right down here, I can bring the wigs to you. Just point at which ones you'd like to try on. I'll fit the wig to you, then voila, you can look at the new you in the mirror."

The woman put her hand on Ribby's back and led her to the chair. Ribby sat while the woman cranked the chair lower and lower. Ribby scooched down further to accommodate.

"What do you do?" the woman asked as she ran her fingers through Ribby's hair. "I mean, how do you make a living? You really want a wig to suit your lifestyle. Oh, your hair is lovely by the way."

"Uh, thank you. I work at the library. I'd like a blond wig. Short, like the one in the window. There."

"Oh my, that is an interesting choice. It's our most popular blond wig. You know the saying, blonds have more fun."

The woman had a box behind the counter filled with wigs exactly like the one in the window. She brought it over and began to tie Ribby's real hair up.

"I changed my mind," Angela said. She pointed up, "I'd like to try on that one."

What? What are you doing?

The other one is common. I want something special.

Fair enough.

The wig had bangs swept across the forehead and flipped under at the back. It was shoulder length and felt quite stiff.

Definitely not.

Agreed.

What about that one?

It was noticeably short with a part on the left side, but it was staggered. The bangs were feathered, the style layered all over and the hair ended just under the earlobes. The minute the woman put it on, both Ribby and Angela loved it. It was a total contrast to Ribby's everyday look.

I can't believe it, I look beautiful.

Of course, you do, Angela.

"Perfect! Wrap it up!" Ribby said. "I have to get back to work."

Now all we need are some new clothes!

Ribby spent the afternoon working on the computer. She emailed first offender patrons who were late in returning their books. Repeat offenders required a phone call.

After work, they went to the mall and bought a few things. It was late so Ribby had to catch an Uber to get to the hospital on time.

She threw herself into entertaining the children. Mikey's absence still hung in the air, never-the-less the children managed to smile and even laugh a little.

On the way home on the bus, the wind caught Ribby's jacket and pushed her along.

Why aren't we going to our real home?

It's only Monday, we don't want Mom to get suspicious.

Okay. I'll go along with this charade.

Shhh.

Ribby turned the handle and opened the front door to Martha's house.

A man's voice broke into laughter.

Ribby listened for a few moments and heard cutlery clicking against the plates. Her stomach growled. She hadn't eaten anything all day.

In the kitchen John MacGraw dipped his bread into his half-empty bowl. Martha spooned stew into Scamp's bowl, and he lapped it up.

When she entered the kitchen Ribby looked over at Martha who was smiling. When John was around, sometimes Martha seemed like a different person. Of all the beaus her mom brought home, John was the most decent. He brought out the best in her mom who seemed to want him to think they were close.

"Hello, Ma. Hello to you too, John."

"Join us," Martha cooed, patting the seat of the chair nearest to her. Before Ribby could sit down, Martha jumped up. "Wait! I have something to show you first. It's a gift from John."

"It can wait until after dinner," John said, encouraging them both to sit down with a firm voice.

"It certainly smells good," Ribby said as Martha took her hand and pulled her out of the kitchen.

"Ta-dah!" Martha said. It was a new portable phone with a very long extension.

"Wow, that's awesome."

"It sure is, now let's get back into the kitchen. We don't want to keep John waiting."

"Your mom is a great cook," John said as soon as they sat down.

"Thank you, for the phone."

"No worries, it's about time you had one here. Makes it easier for me to get in touch," John said.

Martha dished some more stew into John's bowl. "I'm not sure if I mentioned it to you before, John. Ribby spends her Monday evenings entertaining sick children at the hospital." She ladled some into Ribby's bowl. "How was Mikey today?" Without waiting for an answer, "Mikey is Ribby's favourite, he--"

Ribby burst into tears. She hadn't cried for Mikey before. Now she couldn't stop. The tears kept flowing, dripping down her cheeks, into the bowl of stew.

"Snap out of it, girl," Martha said with a raised voice. She glanced at John to see if he noticed. Satisfied he hadn't, she patted Ribby's hand and cooed. "What is the matter? Us with company and all, and you there blubbering like a baby. You get a hold of yourself." She pressed a nail into the back of Ribby's hand and whispered, "You're embarrassing John."

"Ouch," Ribby said, pulling her hand away and continuing sobbing.

"Don't worry about me," John said. "A good cry never hurt anyone. This is your home, Ribby, and you can cry if you want to."

Ribby started to laugh. Not chuckle, but to laugh. In her head a tune was playing: *It's my home and I can cry if I want to, cry if I want to, cry if I want to.* "Mikey's dead."

Chapter Nine

"Angela invited me for the entire weekend," Ribby said at breakfast the next morning.

"It's good timing Ribby, good timing. John and I are spending the weekend together. We have plans."

Ribby sighed in relief.

"Have a wonderful time and…" She grabbed hold of Ribby's wrist. "I want to say how sorry John and I were last night, to hear about little Mikey. I don't want you to get all misty-eyed again, but I'm proud of you. I hope, you have a good time this weekend. You deserve it."

Ribby, startled by her mother's kind words threw her arms around her neck.

"Well then," she said patting her daughter's back.

They separated and Ribby made her way to the bus stop. Her day was becoming less and less like Groundhog Day.

What a crock. How could you hug her after everything she has said and done to you? How could you? Made my skin crawl.

She was sincere.

You are sooooo naïve!

***

Wearing the new wig and dark sunglasses, Angela was determined to go on a shopping spree.

But we can't afford it.

That's what credit is for.

I still have to pay it back.

Chill, it'll be fine.

Angela tried on the most un-Ribby-esque outfits, maxing out her credit card.

Honestly, no more spending.

Okay, okay, but don't we look fab?!

Ribby admitted she could no longer recognize herself.

You're there. You're the window and I'm the frame.

Heads turned as she walked along the promenade. There were catcalls and whistles.

She popped into a different nightclub closer to the waterfront. The bouncer checked Ribby's I.D. He gave the picture a double take.

"Are you sure this is you?" he inquired.

"Of course, it is," Ribby replied. "It's a wig."

"Apologies, I didn't mean to offend. Here's a coupon for a free drink."

"Thanks."

I didn't like the way that guy looked at us.

Yeah, it was like he had x-ray vision and could see right through the dress.

What a creep.

Let's just get the free drink and then head on over to the Cat's Eye.

***

Sometime later she arrived at the Cat's Eye and spotted Nigel sitting on his own.

I don't think he recognizes us.

Why should he? We're wearing dark glasses and a blond wig.

Angela ordered a Martini.

The mere thought of alcohol made Ribby's stomach feel queasy.

Nigel glanced over at Angela. She acknowledged him with a wink, then tossed back the Martini. She ordered another one.

"Would you like to dance?" he asked.

Nigel put his arms around Angela's waist and held her close to him. He gazed into Angela's dark sunglasses.

Angela slipped her hand onto Nigel's right buttock. She rocked him back and forwards against her. The two gyrated in the dark to the pulsating disco sound. Before the song ended, they were kissing. They forgot they were in a public place. Nigel took her hand and led her out of the club.

There were no words, as the passion between them was too great. They walked a few steps, and then Angela pushed him against the stonewall and kissed him once again.

They walked on further, passing the 7-11. Clutching each other, kissing, Angela's lipstick was on his collar and across the side of his face. Both looked like they had been in a battle.

When they arrived at Ribby's place, Nigel realized who Angela was. She took his hand and led him upstairs.

"Uh, wait a minute," Nigel said. "Is this some kind of a game?"

"Of course not," Angela said, unfastening the buttons on his shirt, kissing down his chest. "Come on."

"I don't know what's up with you," Nigel said. "I..."

"Oh, shut up! And they say women talk too much!" she said as they tore each other's clothes off and fell onto the bed.

After, Nigel picked up his clothes and slipped out before Angela awoke.

Ribby did not remember leaving the nightclub.

Angela remembered every single detail.

Chapter Ten

RIBBY BALUSTRADE'S CHILDHOOD HAD not been a happy one. She was a lonely only child who would have benefitted from a two-parent household. Since she never knew her father, she had to imagine him. She saw him as a cross between Atticus Finch's *To Kill A Mockingbird* character and Gregory Peck's real-life persona.

When Ribby asked about her father, Martha changed the subject.

Ribby went back to reading *To Kill A Mockingbird*. "You never really understand a person until you consider things from his point of view...until you climb into his skin and walk around in it."

After numerous questions about her father and no answers, Ribby hatched a plan. She'd climb up into what her mother called the 'No-Go-Zone'—the attic—and investigate like Nancy Drew did. Unfortunately, all she discovered up there were wall-to-wall creepy-crawlers, mostly spiders. Plus, a sickly stench of old dusty and musty forgotten boxed items unrelated to her father.

Sneaking back down, she heard her mother's shoes clicking on the front porch. Realising she had forgotten to close the attic door, Ribby panicked. She moved the ladder back into its original position, planning to fix it later. She hoped her mother wouldn't notice.

When they sat down to dinner, Ribby prayed over and over again that her mother wouldn't notice. She told God that she would never say or do any bad thing for the rest of her life. She vowed to give up her favourite toy, a blond, fair-complexioned doll named Anna.

Martha hung up her coat then went straight into the kitchen. She sat down. Ribby set the kettle to boiling and served her mother a cup of coffee. Martha sipped, careful not to smudge her lippy.

Ribby observed this nuance. The preservation of lippy meant Martha was going out again. She thanked God for hearing her and her pulse slowed.

"So, what did you get up to today then?" Martha asked. "Did you finish your homework?"

"Nearly, Mama, nearly," Ribby replied bending forward to top up her mother's cup of coffee.

"By the way, what were you doing up in the No-Go-Zone, my girl?" Martha asked, steadying Ribby's shaking hand as she poured.

Ribby did not make eye contact with her mother. A few seconds later, urine splashed down her legs, onto her shoes, onto the floor, and she began to cry.

"Confound it, Ribby. Now look what you've done! Peed all over my floor. You get the mop and clean it up. Don't worry about tidying yourself, clean this up! What is a mother supposed to do with a daughter who tells lies? What is a mother to do with a daughter who pees all over her nice clean floor?"

Ribby mopped frantically. The backward and forward sloshing gave her time to think. The cold feeling of the urine on her skin made her shiver. When the floor was spotless again, Ribby returned the mop to its place and made to go upstairs and change.

"Not so fast, my girl," Martha said, grabbing her daughter by the hair and dragging her to the ladder. "Can't leave that open all night, now, can we? Creepy crawlies you know. Now, you get up there," Martha said as she pushed her daughter in an upward motion.

Ribby flailed her arms. Afraid to go up. Afraid to fall down.

When she reached the top Martha laughed. "In fact, since you like it up there so much, you ought to spend the night. You go in, my girl." Martha climbed the ladder behind her. "You think about what a No-Go-Zone means," Martha hooted as she closed the trap door. The ladder swayed under Martha's weight. When her high heels touched the floor, they clicked away then stopped. Ribby was already crying. "I'll put the lock on and turn out the light. Are you listening?"

Ribby sobbed even more loudly.

"In case you're wondering, there aren't only spiders up there. There are also little furry rats!"

Ribby screamed and pounded on the door, begging her mother to let her out. Pleading. Swearing she would never disobey her again. There was no answer.

Outside a car door slammed. Martha and one of her beaus sped away.

Something furry brushed past her leg and she ran, stumbled, and hit her head. She called to her mother again. Still, no answer.

When Martha returned, she said, "Don't go up there again. I mean, never."

"Yes, Mama," Ribby said, and she never did.

The memory of being trapped in the attic. The humiliation of wetting her pants. All the guilt and shame flooded back with a vengeance. The same traumatic memory. Forcing Ribby to relive it, over and over again.

Your mother is a total and complete COW.

She meant well. It was a lesson learned.

My foot means well, and I'd put it right up her backside if she tries anything like that ever again.

I'm glad you're in my corner now.

It no longer surprised or shocked Ribby, what Angela knew.

And don't you ever forget it!

Chapter Eleven

ANGELA WAS COMPLETELY BAFFLED by Ribby's loyalty to Martha. Living in Ribby's mind with a firsthand account of Martha's cruelty was excruciating.

Angela used her strength of internal dialogue, to help Ribby face the past. She encouraged Ribby to clench her fists. This focussed her energy in the moment. The action worked at first, even when Ribby was having a bad dream or a flashback.

Later, Angela attempted to gather the bad memories and push them back. Away. So far into Ribby's mind that they were no longer reachable. In theory it was a good idea, in reality, Angela couldn't block them out.

The only way out, seemed to be the obvious. To take Ribby away from the situation once and for all. Somewhere, far away where Martha couldn't take advantage of her, or damage her anymore. Angela thought it had to be a clean break. She awaited the moment when the timing would be right.

Good things come to those who wait.

After another week at the Martha abode, Angela was happy to be heading out to party. She was wearing the blond wig, dark sunglasses, and a red sleeveless dress. In her new outfit, she felt powerful, invincible. She was also determined not to let anything get in the way of having fun.

On the walk toward the nightclub, a group of teenage boys whistled, and catcalled. They were mere adolescents, but boys who should have known better.

Angela pulled the nearest one to her by the front of his shirt. "Come near me again, **any of you**, and I'll rip your balls off and feed them to you for breakfast. Got it?"

The boys scampered.

Angela laughed, smoothing the front of her dress and checking to make sure she hadn't broken a nail. She lit a cigarette and continued walking along the beach and into the pub.

Fierce.

Wow, what's up? That was more than a little O.T.T.

Boys become men. They ought to learn respect.

They ran like you were Bellatrix Lestrange!

Not in this wig!

Arriving at the nightclub, Ribby sidled up to the bar and ordered a drink. She sipped reluctantly. Angela took over and tossed the Martini back. She ordered another, catching the eye of a very fit bouncer in the entryway.

Let's wait another minute or two for Nigel.

He won't remember us anyway.

Oh, he'll remember me alright.
Two Martinis later.
Let's go; there's nothing happening here.
Patience, my dear friend, patience.
The bouncer parted the younglings coming down the stairs on his way over to where Ribby was sitting.

"How're you doing?" he said trying too hard to be sexy.

"Very well, thank you," Ribby said.

Shut up Rib—let me handle this one. "Actually, this place is Bores-ville tonight."

"Yes, it's a little like Sesame Street in here, isn't it?" the bouncer said before introducing himself as "Ed; Ed the Bouncer."

"I'm Angela."

"Nice to know you, Angela," Ed said as he tried to look down the front of her dress. "Uh, if you're looking for a good time, hang around until 2. I get off work then. We can go out somewhere?"

"Uh, thanks for the offer," Ribby said, "but, we have to...."

"I can be back around 2:30," Angela said. "Where should we meet?"

Ed was extremely specific about the secluded spot on the beach.

Angela hoped he was as good as he looked.

***

I CAN'T BELIEVE YOU made a date with that goon. We're absolutely and completely NOT going.

Rib, don't you worry about it. Chill. Have a nap. I'll fill you in later. Off you go now kiddo, nightie night.

At 2:30, Angela waited on the beach. She had changed into a black dress.

Ed the Bouncer swaggered into view and she called out to him. He stumbled toward her.

"You're pissed."

"A wee bit, but not enough." He pushed her to the ground, tore at her dress and fell on top of her.

"Easy now boy, easy," Angela said trying to gain control.

"Come on, baby. I promised to show you a good time." He pressed his mouth onto hers.

"Ouch," Angela said, "not so rough baby. I don't like it rough."

But Ed didn't seem to care. His hands ripped and tore.

"Didn't your mama teach you any manners?" Angela said, as she pushed him back with her fingers splayed.

"Women like me want a guy to be kind; gentle." She pounded on his chest.

He grabbed her wrists in his massive hands and straddled her. "Some women do, and some women don't." He laughed. "I had you pegged from the minute I saw you. Sitting at the bar with your dress sky high. Eyeing every guy who came in the door. Desperate for it. Gagging for it."

"Wait a minute," Angela said, struggling to break free. "I do want you, but not here. I'd like it to be you know, a bit more romantic for my first time."

Ed froze.

She continued. "Have you ever seen the movie *From Here to Eternity* with Burt Lancaster and Deborah Kerr? You know the one where they do it as the surf comes in?"

He leaned in closer. "Sure, it's a classic." He leaned down and kissed her neck. "Less talk, eh, babe?"

"Come closer to the water, like in the movie, know what I mean?" Angela whispered. "Take me there, I want you there."

Ed stopped. She pushed away and stood up.

She reached into her handbag then dropped it and ran for the water. She glanced over her shoulder. He watched her.

At the water's edge she lifted the hem of her dress.

Ed tore off his shirt and raced in her direction dropping his jeans along the way.

When he lunged at her, the key she held went straight into his eye socket. He screamed then wailed as his groin connected with her knee. She cringed at the squelching sound when she pulled the key out of his eye. As the blood flowed down his face he sobbed and rolled around holding his groin area. She stabbed the key into the side of his neck, connecting with an artery. Blood spurted like water from a fireman's hose.

She moved a few steps from the body and dipped her toes into the water. She glanced back at him every now and again. Until he stopped moving. She went back and listened to see if he was dead: he was. Finally. She rolled him, like a sack of potatoes, deeper and deeper into the water. With every push, the corpse seemed lighter and lighter.

Archimedes was right.

When he was as far out as she could manage, she swam back to the shore and gathered up her clothes and redressed.

She left his things where he'd dropped them.

As the new day's sun turned the sky a fiery red, Angela returned to the water.

She scanned the shoreline and saw no sign of him. She dipped the key into the water to rinse the blood off, then skipped home. After a long shower, she slept like a baby.

Chapter Twelve

RIBBY OPENED HER EYES. The sun streaming in made her cringe. A familiar feeling of déjà vu made her sit up. She stretched and yawned, wondering why she felt so awful. She couldn't remember anything after sitting at the bar.

She clambered out of bed and set the coffee to brew while she showered and dressed. She spotted her dress on the floor, crumpled. She picked it up and sand fell to the floor. She shrugged and tossed it into the laundry basket.

As she stirred sugar into her coffee, she thought about the dress and the sand. She tried to remember the night before, but nothing came.

She checked outside her door for the newspaper. She glanced at the headline as she picked up her coffee. She tucked the newspaper under her arm and pulled back the glass doors and was assaulted by sounds of chaos. Police cars. Ambulances. Fire trucks. The Press. A crowd of onlookers. Bedlam and not far from her home. The police had blocked most of the area with sand barriers. Near the water's edge another area had been cordoned off with flags.

Angela had a fairly good idea what all the fuss was about.

I've got to see what's happening.

Perhaps it's a closed set for a reality program. Or a film.

Oh, that would be exciting. I'm going to have a look.

Ribby dressed and went to the beach. She wormed her way into the crowd and asked an elderly lady what happened.

"Dead," the woman said. "Found dead. Snapping turtles must've gotten to him. What a sight!" She wiped her brow with a handkerchief.

Duuun dun duuun dun dun dun dun dun dun dun BOM BOM...

Jaw's theme? Must you? She said it was a snapping turtle.

"Oh, my goodness, poor man."

I did it my way.

You, shh. Please.

The policeman had a megaphone. He asked everyone to disperse unless they had evidence to present.

Duuun dun duuun dun dun dun dun dun dun dun, BOM BOM...

Snapping turtle.

***

R IBBY, FRIGHTENED BY THE chaos surrounding her new home, returned to her old home.
Why are you going back there? Stay here and see what's going on.
No, I want to get away from the noise.
What if Martha and one of her beaus is noisier with the bouncy-bouncy?
Ewww. I'll cross that bridge when I get to it.
She opened the blinds in the living room. Nothing outside stirred, not even a breeze. The clock ticked away behind her in sync with her heartbeat. It was quiet, almost too quiet. She closed the blinds.
She reached for the remote and turned the television on. She clicked around but found nothing to catch her interest. She flipped through a magazine, then chose a book from the shelf. Neither held her attention. She went into the kitchen and made herself a cup of tea.
On her way back, the front doorbell rang. She opened the door to find herself face-to-face with their

neighbour. Mrs. Engle was armed with two casserole dishes.

"Hello there, Ribby," Mrs. Engle said pushing her way in. "Well, your ma told me you had room in the fridge for this." Mrs. Engle placed the casserole on the table, opened the fridge, and leaned in to spy a spot.

"I've been away all weekend. I haven't even had a chance to look in the fridge."

"There's plenty of room. I need to…" Mrs. Engle didn't finish. She shifted everything around and then put her goods in. "I'll be back to get it in a few days, Rib. My great-great-uncle Phil died. They're all coming to mine. They eat a lot. Your Ma said whatever I could fit in would be fine with her."

"I'm sorry to hear about your uncle. Of course, you're always welcome." Ribby began walking toward the front door hoping her neighbour would follow.

"You are a dear, Rib," Mrs. Engle hesitated, stood stock still. "Do you still entertain those dear little ones at the Hospital?"

"I sure do. Without fail every Monday."

They moved to the front door.

"Oh, by the by, your mom said she would be away until Tuesday or Wednesday. She and Tom, or Jerry, not sure which one, went up the coast for a few days. He's asthmatic, don't you you know? His doctor suggested getting out of the city. Your mom went along for company, and she took Scamp."

Ribby crossed her arms. "Mom off on an extended holiday. Only wish I'd known, as I could have stayed at my friend Angela's house a little longer."

Mrs. Engle's eyebrows went up. "Well, she didn't have your friend's phone number."

"Thanks for letting me know." Ribby opened the door and followed Mrs. Engle out onto the porch.

In the dark, mosquitoes buzzed, and crickets chirped. Her crossed arms proved little protection against the coolness of the night air.

"Night, Ribby, and thanks again."

"Good night, Mrs. Engle." Ribby closed the front door and locked it.

She's a crazy old boot.

She's been our neighbour since I was a little girl.

Oh, the stories she could tell.

She's not a gossip, like some of the other neighbours.

Life in the suburbs.

Yes, it's very dull most of the time.

It's way too quiet around here and I'm thirsty. I mean for a drink. A real drink.

Mom probably has some Jack Daniels, but she'll miss it if we have a drop.

Come on, live dangerously.

Ribby acquiesced, poured a jigger and tossed it back. It burned on the way down. It was a good burn.

More please.

We better replace this before Mom notices.

Think about it...who paid for it? We did.

Yeah, but the whole bottle. My stomach aches and my head spins.

Time for beddy-bye. Sleep it off.

On the way upstairs, Ribby hung onto the railing to steady herself. In her room she threw her clothes off and fell into bed. She sat up, remembering she hadn't locked the door. She swayed over to it, locked it, then crashed back into bed.

Better safe than sorry.

Soon Ribby was sound asleep. She dreamed she was Deborah Kerr making love to Burt Lancaster in *From Here to Eternity.*

The waves crashed over their bodies as it carried them out to the sea. They were locked together in a deep embrace. Then, Lancaster looked up at her, only he wasn't Burt Lancaster anymore. He was a stranger. His eye had a key sticking out of it. There was blood on her hands.

Ribby woke up screaming. She jumped out of bed and ran to the bathroom to wash the blood from her hands. As she turned the faucet on, she glanced at her fingers. The blood was no longer there. Angela dreamed on.

Chapter Thirteen

*T*AKE A DAY OFF.

Are you asking me to call in sick? I'm not calling in sick.

At least ditch the hospital gig. I can't face going there today.

I'll think about it.

As the day progressed, Ribby had an uneasy feeling.

For the first time ever, she called the hospital and cancelled her performance. "I'll make it up and do two performances another week," she said, to make herself feel better.

Thanks, Rib.

I'm not doing it because you asked me to, I cancelled because I need to go home.

Why? You mean to Martha's? She's not even there.

I don't know why. I just know I have to go.

Whatever!

After work she caught the bus, soon arriving at her house. There, sitting on the front porch was a woman. A stranger. As she neared, she heard sobs and the woman looked up. It was her mother's sister, Aunt

Tizzy who she hadn't seen in years. Ribby didn't know what happened between them, but she did know that Aunt Tizzy swore never to set foot on her sister's doorstep again. And yet, there she was.

What's she doing here?

No idea. I'm sure she'll tell us in her own time.

That'll be interesting. Not.

Ribby reminisced about their last meeting. It was on her seventh birthday. Aunt Tizzy had made her a special Barbie doll cake. It had a pink dress made of icing, with bows all around it made from maraschino cherries and coconut. Barbie's body was in the centre of the cake. After everyone had their slices, Ribby as the birthday girl got to pull Barbie out. She was hers to keep. Aunt Tizzy had purchased several outfits for Barbie. Only thing was, Aunt Tizzy had forgotten to wrap Barbie up before she put her into the cake. For weeks icing, coconut and cake fell out of the doll's appendages.

"Come on in, Aunt Tizzy," Ribby said after removing herself from her Aunt's vice-like grip. "What happened? Is Mom, okay?"

"This has nothing to do with Martha," she said followed by another crying fit.

We don't need this. Tell her to go to a hotel.

I can't do that, she's family.

She's a Drama Queen.

Once inside, Ribby offered Tizzy a cup of tea. She declined.

"Let's take your mind off things and watch some television. Are you hungry? I could order in or make something?"

"If you don't mind, I'd like to cook dinner for you," Aunt Tizzy suggested. "It'll take my mind off everything, more than watching tv." She walked into the kitchen. "An apron?"

Ribby opened the drawer and pulled out one of Martha's aprons.

Aunt Tizzy fastened it around herself. "What do you like to eat?"

"Surprise me," Ribby said. "If you can't find something, just shout."

"Will do."

Even with the television on, Ribby could hear her aunt milling about in the kitchen and humming.

Some time later, she heard plates and cutlery being set upon the table and went in, to ask if she could help.

"No, just sit yourself down," Aunt Tizzy said. "Spaghetti Bolognaise and garlic bread with cheese coming right up. What would you like to drink? Have you any wine?"

"Just water. I'll check for wine."

"No, that's fine. I don't need anything. Just thought you might like some."

They chatted and enjoyed a lovely dinner, then tidied up.

"I'm exhausted," Aunt Tizzy said. "The couch is fine. I don't want to be any trouble."

"No trouble at all, you can sleep in my mom's room."

"Are you sure she won't mind?"

"No, I think she'll be glad you stopped by."

She'd be surprised to see her.

Hours later, Ribby tossed and turned in bed. Across the hallway her Aunt's sporadic sobs rang out.

On the to buy list, one pair of noise blocking headphones.

Good idea!

That's what I'm here for.

Chapter Fourteen

In the dream, Ribby floated high upon a cloud. Everything was black and white except for her red dress. It was like a wedding dress with a long train which flowed over the cloud edges.

She floated into her apartment, and watched herself making love to someone not once, but twice. Once she drifted off to sleep, the man dressed and left the building.

Out on the street, she was now Angela. Walking for blocks and blocks, then into the ocean. Deeper and deeper she went, as the water rose up and over her head.

Ribby wanted to reach down and grab her, to save her, but she couldn't. She called out to Angela from upon her cloud, tossing down the train of her dress, begging Angela to grab hold of it. But Angela didn't seem to hear her.

Angela was fully under. Only bubbles rose to the surface.

Into the water Ribby dove from her cloud.

When she found Angela, she floated face down.

Ribby became Angela, Angela became Ribby and together they broke through the surface.

Chapter Fifteen

When Ribby awoke, voices on the radio whispered up the stairs. She wondered if her mother had returned.

She dressed and went downstairs where Aunt Tizzy was seated like death warmed over at the kitchen table.

The coffee percolator was bubbling away. Aunt Tizzy had already set the table with cereal bowls, toast, and jam.

"Good morning," Ribby said. "Did you sleep well?"

Aunt Tizzy nodded without saying a word.

Ribby would have asked her about the reason for her visit but decided not to. She didn't want her aunt to start wailing again. She'd share why she had come when she was ready.

I wish she'd get on with it. She didn't come all this way for nothing.

Shhhh. Don't be rude.

After a few moments of silence, Ribby went out onto the front porch to collect the newspaper. The headlines read, "Autopsy Complete—Murdered!"

She skimmed over the story about Jason Edward Thompson the identity of the man found dead near her apartment. She zeroed in on the picture and recognized him: it was Ed the Bouncer. He was a big guy and she wondered how such a thing could happen in the neighbourhood where she lived. It was sad, for him to die so young and even though she didn't know him, she felt sorry for his family.

Ribby put the newspaper onto the kitchen table and poured herself a cup of coffee. She turned her attention to her aunt. "When you're ready to talk, I'm here for you."

"I had nowhere else to go," Aunt Tizzy said. "My husband left me for another woman. My daughter hates me. She says her father wouldn't have gone looking for someone else if I'd been a better wife to him. Jenny is twenty-five, has never been away from home and she's out there alone maybe even living on the streets. I had to come and see if I could find her and bring her home. Her friend said she was fairly sure Jenny was headed this way. I was hoping she might contact you. Have you heard anything from her?"

Oh brother.

"I'm sorry, but I was away all weekend and my mom's been away too. Does she have our address?"

"She might have taken it from my phone. She doesn't have much money, not even a credit card. My husband blames me. He's worried as much as I am, but he's got his bit on the side to comfort him." Her voice quavered.

Sounds like an episode of The Young and the Restless. Behave.

"You must be so worried. I'm sorry, but I need to get dressed and go to work. If you want, we could meet for lunch and talk more?" Ribby hurried up the stairs as she continued. "I work at the Library. She might come by to use the free wi-fi. Lots of people do. You could venture into the city too and look for her."

"I'd rather stay here, but she has my cell phone number."

"Have you contacted the police?"

"I called them. They have my number and Gordon's. What else can I do?"

"Do you have a recent photo of Jenny?" She pulled her dress over her head and then added, "I'll make some flyers, and we can post them around town."

"Good thinking. I'm so glad I came here," Aunt Tizzy said.

Ribby ran a brush through her hair. She hurried back down to the kitchen. Aunt Tizzy rummaged through her purse, withdrew a photograph of her daughter, and handed it to her. She told her aunt to make herself at home and went out, pausing momentarily to glance back at the house.

Her aunt waved to her like a lost child from behind the open blinds.

Chapter Sixteen

RIBBY DIDN'T GO TO work because Angela called in sick.

Angela went to the apartment and changed into her swimsuit. While the direct sunlight was on her balcony, she caught a few rays. When it moved away, she threw a sundress over the swimsuit, packed a bag, and made her way toward the beach. Angela liked the hustle and bustle, the hum, and the sounds of the city. Aunt Tizzy's constant wailing and whining was driving her mad.

As she passed by the school grounds, she spotted a little girl crying. The child looked up, and then looked down again like she didn't want to draw attention to herself.

"What's the matter?" Angela asked.

"Nothing," the child replied.

The school bell sounded, and the little girl wiped away her tears and straightened out her dress.

Angela watched, hoping she had helped in some way by stopping.

The child turned toward her and stuck her tongue out.

Cheeky Little Madam.

Angela bought a copy of *Gone With The Wind* to read on the beach.

"It makes me cry," the lady behind the till said.

"Rhett Butler could eat crackers in my bed any old time," Angela replied.

The sand was scorching hot as it squished through the sides of her sandals. She loved the beach but getting the sand everywhere—not so much.

She spread out her blanket, laid on her belly, and cracked open her book. She watched as couples walked by hand-in-hand swooning over each other. The seagulls swooped around her head taking aim as if her blonde wig was a target.

Angela fell asleep listening to the sounds of the gulls and the waves crashing upon the shore. When she awoke, it was nearly 5 p.m. and she gathered herself and her things and put them into her bag. The sun gave no warmth. Her skirt twisted around her legs in the wind.

It wasn't her usual night to perform at the hospital. This was a make-up gig.

Ribby created a flyer and printer off some copies with the intention of posting a few along the way, and on the hospital bulletin board.

Why do we have to keep performing for those brats?

#1. They aren't brats. They're little angels, who've been dealt a bad hand. #2. I will do anything to make them smile, to see them laugh. To lessen the burden on their families. #3. If you don't like it, you can lump it.

   That's me told.
   Exactly.
   For now.

***

After the hospital performance, Ribby went home. Sitting in front of her house, was the white Attics-R-Us van. She glanced at the window, noticed the blinds were open and ran up the stairs. A blood-curdling scream rang out.

Ribby's heartbeat so heavily she thought it was going to break out of her chest. She raced along the hallway, into the kitchen where she found Aunt Tizzy on the floor, pounding her fists against the bulky form of the Attics-R-Us man.

Ribby didn't hesitate when she reached into the cutlery drawer, coming out with a large knife. She lunged and stabbed the knife into his back.

He fell forward, making a ghastly gurgling noise. Ribby pulled the knife out and blood flowed.

Aunt Tizzy trapped under the hefty man's flab, gave his body a shove.

Ribby helped her to stand and the two of them stood back as the blood puddle expanded.

Aunt Tizzy screamed.

Ribby screamed.

Like two headless chickens they ran about the kitchen crying and screeching.

STOP.

Ribby obeyed and stood still.

Aunt Tizzy continued racing about.

STOP. You're making me dizzy, Aunt Tizzy.

She did stop. She looked at the body, at the pool of blood. She lifted her dress. More blood. She tried to wipe it away.

"I need to…" Aunt Tizzy went to the sink and vomited into it.

Ribby listened to the sounds of the upchucking and the ticking of the clock. She drummed her fingers on the kitchen table.

Calm. I'm calm now.

Jesus, Ribby.

I had to save Aunt Tizzy. I had to. Maybe he's not dead. Maybe I should call an ambulance?

No ambulance. Check for a pulse.

Ribby picked up his wrist.

Don't you need a watch for this?

Angela took over.

Dead as a doornail.

I killed someone, I killed someone!

Yes, you did. You surprised me. Now, we need a plan.

I need to speak to my Aunt first.

No, we need a plan. Aunt Tizzy can wait.

Aunt Tizzy attempted to sit down, but instead of doing so she screamed and ran upstairs.

We need to flip him over.

What about the knife?

Under the sink, get the rubber gloves. Then find something to put it in like a newspaper, blanket, or towel. Something that won't be missed.

Ribby found the gloves and put them on. She grabbed a newspaper out of the recycling bin in which she wrapped the knife, plus a blanket and a towel from the linen cupboard.

Now, back at the body, she bent down and gave it a shove. It bounced right back again. She made another attempt, this time pushing the body with the motion and holding it with her leg. She retched but managed to keep the contents of her stomach down. She flipped him the rest of the way. His penis flopped, and his head hit the leg of the table with a dull thwunk. She threw the blanket over him, convinced he was dead now.

From upstairs Aunt Tizzy called out, "Who the hell was that S.O.B. anyway?"

***

Aunt Tizzy returned to the kitchen. "We should call the police," she said.

Absolutely not.

She's right, we've got to call the police.

Do you want to go to prison for killing that rapist son of a bitch?

I'll explain. I was saving Aunt Tizzy.

But how will you explain why he was here in the first place?

"Uh, Aunt Tizzy. How did he get in? Why did you let him in?" Ribby inquired.

"He knocked on the door and came right in, like he was expected. I figured he was a friend of Martha's so offered him a cup of coffee. The minute I turned my back on him, he pushed me down onto the floor and...and..." she put her hands over her face and sobbed.

Ribby comforted her with, "It's going to be okay. I promise. We'll figure it out."

We need to get rid of the body.

Get rid of it! How? Why?

Because you killed him and because his van is still parked in front of the house.
The van. I forgot about the van.
We have to get him out of here.
He's way too heavy to lift. We have a wheelbarrow.
Good idea. We'll put him in the wheelbarrow.
"Aunt Tizzy," Ribby patted her hand. "Why don't you make us a nice cup of tea? I'm going outside for a minute...you can make us a cup of tea, yes?"
"You're going to leave me alone—with that?"
"I'll only be a few minutes. Make the tea, take your mind off it. He can't hurt you now."
Once outside, Ribby unlocked the shed and pulled the wheelbarrow out. She pushed it, wheels screeching across the lawn. She tried to lift it up the stairs, but even empty it was too difficult. She turned herself and it around. Walking backwards she pulled until it bumped up the steps onto the front porch. Exhausted, she opened the front door and continued pushing the wheelbarrow along the hallway and into the kitchen.
Ask her to help you. I mean getting him into it.
I will. We need to get rid of his body before the sun comes up. "And what about his van?"
"What van?" Aunt Tizzy asked.
Oops. I actually said that didn't I?
Yepper.
"He left his van outside," Ribby said. She closed the front door behind her.

"Let's get rid of the body and the van at the same time," Aunt Tizzy suggested.

Now she's getting into the spirit of things.

Oh, brother.

Just when they were getting ready to shift the body onto the wheelbarrow, they were interrupted by a knock on the front door.

"Who could that be?" Aunt Tizzy whispered.

Ribby tiptoed to the door and peered into the keyhole. It was Mrs. Engle armed with large trays of food in each hand. She must've knocked with her elbow. Ribby looked down at herself; she had blood stains all over her clothes.

"Yoo-hoo, Ribby. It's me, Mrs. Engle. Just have a couple more things to go into your fridge. I hope you don't mind."

Ribby grabbed her coat off the hook and threw it on, then opened the door. She offered to place the trays into the fridge. She attempted to close the front door with her foot.

"Why thank you, dear," Mrs. Engel said. "Oh, and by the by, I'm going way for a few days, then back for the funeral. I'll let myself in with the spare key if you're not here." She leaned in before she whispered. "Everyone is coming here after the funeral to eat. I never understand why funerals make relatives so hungry. I guess it's a natural reaction, faced with a loved one's mortality. It always has the opposite effect on me."

"I hope everything, uh, goes well for you and your family," Ribby said trying to close the door again.

"Thank you, dear." Mrs. Engel made her way down the stairs and out onto the lawn.

Ribby breathed a sigh of relief, but continued watching,

Mrs. Engle turned around, "By the by, have you heard from Martha?"

"No, no, we haven't," Ribby admitted.

"Oh, I thought…" Mrs. Engel said, looking at the white van.

"I better get these in the fridge for you, Mrs. Engel," Ribby said. "They smell so good and I'm so hungry I could eat them myself right now!"

"You're welcome to leftovers at mine after the get together. It would be a sin to run out of food." She turned and made her way home.

"Whew!" Ribby said. She kicked the front door closed and went into the kitchen. Aunt Tizzy was huddled in the corner, wringing her hands like Lady Macbeth.

Ribby put the casseroles away, tore off the coat and threw it into the hall, then tended to her aunt.

"What are we going to do, Ribby?" Aunt Tizzy said. "We've got to get him out of here. What are we going to do? What? What? What?"

Ribby slapped Tizzy. After the initial shock they came together with a hug.

"I've got a plan, Aunt Tizzy. Don't you worry. But first, I have to get a few things from the shed outside. I'll be right back, I promise."

When Mrs. Engle and her sister were out of sight, Ribby went outside, leaving Aunt Tizzy slumped down on the sofa.

Aunt Tizzy checked for updates on her phone. It pinged with an SMS from her husband. Jenny was with him. She was safe and well.

Tizzy closed her eyes, letting the relief that her daughter was safe rush over her. It had been quite a day.

The overwhelming emotions from the past few days, swelled up within her like a giant wave. Every emotion rose to the surface. The pain, relief, hurt, regret.

Tizzy attempted to stand, but her knees gave out under her. She trembled and shook as she tried to both hide from the truth and come to terms with it.

Chapter Seventeen

RIBBY RETURNED TO THE kitchen. She had with her some tools including: a shovel, an axe, a tarp, a pair of overalls, gardening gloves and a pair of shears. She assessed the situation.

What the heck is all that stuff for?

I just grabbed random things I thought might help.

You sure did.

Ribby put her hands on her hips. "Now let's get him into the wheelbarrow."

"Are you sure he'll fit?" Aunt Tizzy inquired.

Yes, he'll fit.

He's got to, we have no Plan B.

"We'll use the blanket and drag him onto it," Ribby offered. "We don't have to lift him, per se. We'll roll him onto the blanket, and we can adjust as we need to. All we have to do is get him into the wheelbarrow and it will be easy from there."

"Ribby, you're scaring me! It's like, like you've done this before," Aunt Tizzy said. "Uh, you haven't, have you?"

"God no, Aunt Tizzy, but I've read books and I've seen movies. Now let's get moving. Grab a hold of the other end of the blanket and when I get to the count of three, we both shift him. Okay?"

Once they had some momentum, he was easy to roll onto the blanket. Now came the hard part.

"And again. After three."

"Okay Rib, whatever you say."

"1, 2, 3—heave ho!" Ribby said. The dead man's head made a hollow clunking sound as it connected with the metal container.

"One more time!" Ribby commanded, "1, 2, 3—yes!" Ribby said as they deposited the body three quarters of the way onto the wheelbarrow.

"Now, I'll put it upright," Ribby said, "and you tuck in the legs and ...his bits."

"There's no way I'm tucking THAT in anywhere!" Aunt Tizzy said. "It can dangle all the way to Kingdom's come!"

Ribby laughed in spite of herself, and soon Aunt Tizzy fell into fits of laughter too.

The two women were hysterical.

Amateurs.

Angela picked up the wrapped knife and took it upstairs. She wiped off the blood and fingerprints before re-wrapping it. She hid the knife at the very back of Martha's sock drawer.

Angela returned downstairs where she mopped up the bloody mess in the kitchen.

By the time she was finished both Ribby and Tiz were sufficiently calm.

Get on with it, Rib.

"Come on, Aunt Tiz. Let's do this."

"I'm with you."

Hallelujah! We have lift off.

***

"Okay, now we need to find his car keys. Reach into his pockets, Tizzy."

"I will not!"

"Get out of the way," Angela said. She found the keys in his coat pocket.

"Now, we wheel him back to the van and then…"

"You mean take him outside, in this?" Aunt Tizzy asked.

"Yepper. We have no choice, Tiz. We have to do this while it's dark out. We have to get him into his van."

"How will we lift him into it, Rib? It's impossible."

"We have to. We have no choice," Ribby said.

Ribby threw the tarp over the body.

See I told you it would come in handy.

Smarty pants.

Ribby and Aunt Tizzy had to push together to get the dead body to the van. Ribby unlocked the driver's door and opened the back of the van. She pushed a blue button just inside the cargo area and the hydraulic lift groaned downward. Together the two women managed to navigate the wheelbarrow onto the lift and soon the body was in the back of the van.

Ribby went back inside and changed out of her bloody clothes, hiding them in the back of her closet in a plastic bag.

What about the knife?

It's fine, I managed it.

Once outside again, Ribby said, "You have to drive, Aunt Tizzy, because I don't know how."

"But I'm too scared to drive in such a big city! I can't! I won't!"

"Look, we don't have time for this bullshit," Angela interjected. "You're scared of driving when we've got a big fat dead guy here to get rid of! Not to mention nosy neighbours! We need to dispose of his van and his body while it's dark."

"Unless of course you want me to ring the Police and tell them we murdered him, Aunt Tizzy?"

Aunt Tizzy's jaw dropped.

Technically Rib, you murdered him. Just saying.

I know.

Aunt Tizzy close it, or a moth will fly in.

"We'll drive on up to The Bluffs where we can dispose of the body and the van Aunt Tizzy, but you need to snap out of it. You've got to get us there! What do you say?"

Aunt Tizzy nodded.

"Okay then, let's go!" Ribby placed the dead man's keys into the palm of her Aunt's trembling hand.

Chapter Eighteen

Despite everything Aunt Tizzy was a good driver, albeit a nervous one.

On the way, they stopped at a gas station, not far from The Bluffs where Ribby ordered a taxi to pick them up in one hour's time.

As they proceeded into the secluded area, Ribby said, "Put the high beams on, Aunt Tizzy." They inched their way forwards, as the moon on the horizon coaxed them nearer.

"Stop!" Ribby said. When the vehicle lurched to a complete stop, she and Aunt Tizzy got out.

"Woo-ee!" Aunt Tizzy exclaimed. "It sure is a long way down!"

"Don't get too close," Ribby said, "the escarpment is crumbling."

They took a couple of steps back just as the clouds parted and the starlight twinkled. They stood together, shivering, side-by-side with the wind whipping around them. Aunt Tizzy hugged herself.

"It sure is beautiful," Aunt Tizzy said.

"I'll have to bring you up here in the daytime, so you can get the full scope of its beauty."

"I'd like that very much, Ribby. By the way, I forgot to tell you—Jenny is with her father. She texted me a little while ago."

"That's excellent news."

OMG! What is this, The Young and the Restless? Get on with it Rib!

Okay, okay. "Aunt Tizzy, all you have to do is put the van into gear, and once the vehicle is moving forward, jump out. It'll go over the cliff and the snappers will have him for breakfast. Bye bye, fat bastard. Bye bye, fat bastard's van. Bye bye troubles. End of story! Then we can go back to our lives. It'll be our little secret."

"God will know," Aunt Tizzy said.

And me.

"God will understand because it was self-defence. He was raping you, Aunt Tizzy!"

She's getting cold feet Ribby. Do it now.

"God always knows," Aunt Tizzy said as she turned and walked away. She glanced over her shoulder, then opened the door of the van and climbed inside. She pulled the door shut and the engine started. She revved it once, twice, three times. Then headed for the cliff edge.

"JUMP, Aunt Tizzy!"

It was too late. The van kept going. Over.

Ribby ran toward the edge and got there just in time to see the van hit the water.

She tried to scream but nothing came out.

Nothing. Until the vomiting began. She fell to her knees.

Stupid woman.

She didn't have to do that. She didn't have to die.

It was her decision. Her choice.

I keep remembering the Barbie Doll Cake she made for my birthday.

No one can take that memory away. Now let's get the hell out of here.

It hadn't gone to plan. But nothing ever does—not even in the movies. You think Cary Grant is going to stay for the girl, but he doesn't. You think Humphrey Bogart is going to stop Ingrid Bergman from getting on the plane, but he doesn't. Even when you will it to be so, it doesn't happen the way you want it to.

Chapter Nineteen

RIBBY HUNG HER COAT in the entryway and called out, "I'm home, Mom." She made her way to the kitchen, where Martha sat hunched over the table, holding the murder weapon in her hand.

"Been killing pigs, Rib?" she asked holding up the knife. Martha stood.

"I killed the fat bastard," Angela said. "I stabbed him, dead."

Martha opened her mouth, but no words or sounds came out, so Angela continued. "He was a disgusting animal, just a pig, with his cock hanging out of his pants."

"I had to Ma," Ribby interjected. "He was raping Aunt Tizzy!"

She never learns. I was managing this.

Martha placed her left hand on her hip. The right hand holding the knife remained at arm's length. "What on earth are you talking about? Fat bastard? Aunt Tizzy?"

"The guy in the white Attics-R-Us van. He's the fat bastard," Angela said. "And as for your sister, Tizzy, well she was as defenceless as a kitten when he violated her."

"I saved her from him," Ribby said.

Martha turned, like she was going to put the knife down. Then apparently changed her mind and stepped back. "And where are they now? If you killed him where is his body?"

Ribby stared at the knife. "We packed him into his van, drove him over a cliff."

"It was a perfect plan," Angela said. "Until that crazy sister of yours refused to get out of the van and went over the top, too." Angela walked around Martha and plopped herself into a chair in a huff.

Ribby began to speak but changed her mind when the kettle whistled. Martha put down the knife on the kitchen table. She retrieved milk from the fridge and two mugs from the cupboard. The spoons were already on the table, lined up like toy soldiers. As she poured, she said, "Let me see if I get this right then, Rib. My sister came here. Carl Wheeler thought I was open for business and tried it on with Tiz. You stabbed him and then disposed of him. You expect me to believe this? He was an exceptionally large man."

"Damn right he was," Angela said. "Rib—I mean we—put him into the wheelbarrow. That's how we got him out."

"Oh, I see," Martha tsked. "And then you planned to get rid of the body, but Tiz threw a wrench in the plan when she went over too? And what was Tiz doing here anyway? I haven't heard a word from her in years."

"Her husband left her for another woman, younger," Angela said. "Then her daughter ran away. She was a mess."

Martha sat and took a few sips of her tea. "Well, we've got to do something about this knife. It can't stay here in my house." Martha picked up the knife and looked at Ribby who was drinking tea with her right hand. Her left hand was palm down on the table. Martha raised the knife and brought it down, severing Ribby's hand from its friend, the wrist.

The teacup hit the table and bounced. Ribby screamed. Martha grabbed hold of her right hand and pressed it palm down on the table. "You tell me what's going on here and who the hell you are," she demanded. "Because I know you're not my daughter." Martha lifted the knife upwards, so the tip almost connected with Ribby's nose. "Get the hell out of my daughter, whatever you are. Otherwise, I'll tear her apart limb by limb."

"Mama don't. Don't please. Don't!"

"I'm Ribby. Just Ribby," Angela cooed using Ribby's wimpiest voice.

For a second, she thought Martha believed her. Another CHOP, the second hand severed turning Ribby into a two-pronged fountain.

"Die. We all die," Angela sang as Ribby wept and screamed in agony. Angela couldn't feel any pain, nor could she feel any real pleasure. Everything she did, everything she tried to do—it was always Ribby who reaped the benefits. Not this time though. "Poor

Ribby," Angela said. "How will she tend to the sick children at the hospital now?"

Ribby awoke in her apartment with a scream. She checked her right hand. Then her left. Both were still there. Too frightened to get out of bed, she held hands with herself and watched the sunlight draw patterns on the ceiling.

※※※

When she was fully awake, Ribby showered and dressed. She decided to take a walk and clear her head She was grateful it was Sunday. She couldn't face work or the children today.

Once outside, the bad dream moved to the back of her mind. She avoided the beach and the sound of the waves because it brought back memories of Aunt Tizzy.

Before going back, she stopped at a café and ordered a Cappuccino. It tasted so good that she immediately wanted another. While she was waiting to re-order, Nigel passed by. She hadn't seen him for weeks. She wasn't even certain he would remember her.

"Yo! Nigel," Angela called, tapping the window.

He smiled and entered the café. He kissed Ribby on the cheek. She thought this was overfamiliar.

"How the hell have you been?" Nigel asked.

"Busy working," Angela said. "And in need of a little R & R. Want to do something, tonight?"

Nigel looked at his feet. "I have a girlfriend now, so if I do go out, she comes with."

"Poor Nigel," Angela teased, "Not even married and already whipped!"

Nigel threw his head back and laughed. He grabbed hold of Angela's hand and patted it in a brotherly fashion.

"So, what's her name then?" Angela asked. "Or is it a secret?"

"No, Lord no," Nigel said, moving back so a person who'd joined the queue could get in and order. "She's called Anne-Marie."

Angela changed her mind about ordering and started toward the door. "You'll have to introduce us one day."

Nigel moved forward in the queue.

Angela fumed all the way home.

Chapter Twenty

AFTER THE HOSPITAL ON the following evening, Ribby caught the bus home. It was nearly dark when she arrived. The front door stood wide open. Music loud enough to rival the street traffic blasted from within. Cautiously, she made her way up the front stairs when Scamp's paws padded toward her. He jumped up, knocking her over. Martha came along, laughing as the dog licked Ribby's face.

"Get off now, Scamp," Martha said as she pushed his behind off with her foot. She reached her hand out to help Ribby. Once on her feet, Ribby brushed herself down.

"You're nearly skin and bone," Martha said. "Haven't you been eating?"

Ribby grabbed her mother and threw her arms around her neck. Martha hugged back, then let go asking, "Cuppa?"

"You look great, Mom!" Ribby said as they strolled to the kitchen together. "You have an amazing tan."

Martha laughed. "We had a marvellous time. I'd live up there in a minute if I had the cash. Tom was a wonderful host." She moved around the kitchen, setting the kettle to boil, preparing the mugs. "What have you been up to? And whose things are those in my room."

"Aunt Tizzy's."

Martha almost dropped a mug. "My sister is here? Slumming, I suppose. Where is she then? Out shopping?"

"Uh, no, not really," Ribby said. "She came here looking for Jenny." Ribby was having a strange feeling of déjà vu. She shivered and jammed both of her hands into her pockets.

"Well, it sure is a funny thing for her to come all this way. We have a lot of catching up to do for sure."

"I don't know if she'll be back," Ribby stammered. "I think she maybe had to go home. I mean suddenly."

Martha stirred in some sugar. "Without her luggage?" She took a sip. "Have you seen her today?"

"No, I was over at my friend Angela's." She didn't drink the tea or even attempt to. Her hands were still firmly planted inside her pockets.

Martha downed her cup of tea. She pushed her chair back and yawned with her mouth so wide a bus could have gone through it. "I'm off to bed now."

"Night then, Mom," Ribby said. She cleared away her mug and moved around the kitchen until she heard Martha call from the top of the stairs.

"Uh, by the way Rib, I found this," she held up a knife. "It was wrapped up in my sock drawer."

"Maybe Aunt Tizzy murdered someone with it," Angela said as she walked up the steps.

Martha handed her the knife and let out a roaring laugh. "You have quite the imagination. We'll give it a good wash in the morning. Night, night."

Angela accepted the knife from Martha in a new towel.

Why did you use a new towel?

It's for me to know, and for you to find out.

Ribby hid the knife at the back of her closet with her bloody clothes.

Okay, go to sleep then.

Stop talking to me and I will.

Night, Ribby.

Night, Angela.

Chapter Twenty-One

RIBBY FELL INTO A deep sleep. She dreamed she was high up in the clouds where she sat and watched other clouds pass her by. Sometimes the clouds had people riding on them. She recognized someone every now and then. A famous person who seemed to be looking around to see if anyone recognized them.

Seeing Cary Grant smiling and waving at her as his cloud-surfed on by was very strange.

Ribby shouted, "Mr. Grant, oh Mr. Grant, you're my absolute favourite actor!"

"You're very sweet," Cary said, as his cloud continued onwards.

Ribby's eyes followed him until she could no longer see him since most of the clouds had rolled away. Vanished.

With the exception of one huge black cloud which was storming toward her

She wasn't sure what to do, how to propel herself onward. She flapped her arms, but that didn't work. She took in a large breath of air and exhaled into the cloud, but that didn't work either. She didn't have the hang of being on a cloud this time. Previously it had moved when she willed it to, but this time, it wouldn't budge.

The large black cloud floated closer. Ribby sat, then hugged her knees. It was going to rain, and that's why the other cloud riders had gone to find shelter. She felt very alone. If she'd only jumped onto Cary Grant's cloud, then at least she wouldn't be all alone.

BOOM! She fell sideways into the arms of the fluffy cloud. Thunder echoed through the empty sky.

CRACK.

Lightning flashed from the invading black cloud and into Ribby's cloud. She screamed. It was very close. The hair on her arms stood tall with static electricity. Her skin heated, hotter and hotter.

"Stop it!"

"I WILL NOT!" an angry woman's voice screamed.

Lightning struck Ribby's cloud again, this time severing it in half. She rolled to one side and assumed the fetal position. She looked up, to find a woman who looked remarkably like Aunt Tizzy. She wore loose, black garments, not exactly a dress or a cloak, which whipped up and all around her.

"You've done me wrong, and you'll pay. You can't hide forever. Take your chances now—and JUMP!"

"But, Aunt Tizzy," Ribby moaned, "I saved your life!"

"You took my life and sent me to hell! You stupid, stupid girl! Now give up yours and JUMP!"

"But I, I don't want to die."

"Neither did I! Now I'm shunned from Heaven. From God. Destined to hover around here for all eternity."

Another lightning bolt ripped Ribby's cloud into quarters.

The cloud dissipated into a mist, and then nothing at all. Ribby held her nose, like she was jumping into a river instead of falling to her death. She shouted "Shiiiiiiiiiittt!" like Redford and Newman did in *Butch Cassidy and The Sundance Kid* when they leapt from the cliff.

Plummeting into the open arms of nothingness, Ribby fell out of bed and landed with a thump on the floor.

Chapter Twenty-Two

MARTHA WAS DOWNSTAIRS BANGING the pots and pans. Ribby eavesdropped and heard two voices. Her mother had company.

It was Friday morning and Ribby had requested a late start at work. She wanted to hear about her mother's trip before she went to her own place for the weekend.

"Morning, Ma," Ribby said, turning the corner. She spotted John MacGraw reading the newspaper.

Martha stood behind him, reading over his shoulder.

"Morning, John," Ribby said as she poured herself a cuppa and then stood beside the refrigerator.

"Can't find it anywhere. Did you take it, Ribby? My bottle of Jack Daniels? It was here, and it was full."

"Aunt Tizzy drank it," Angela said. "She was in a state and gulped it down to calm her nerves. I'm sure she meant to replace it. I'll get you a new one later."

"Needed it to make our eggs, Rib."

"Yes, nothing like pouring a little bit of Jack Daniels into the eggs. Perfect remedy for a hangover," John said.

"Well, we'll have to do without this morning," Martha said.

"Then no eggs for me, love," John said. "Just another cup of coffee."

Martha brought the pot to the table. "Sit down, daughter. I—we—have something important to talk to you about."

Geez what's this all about?

Ribby studied Martha and John as they exchanged glances. She sat down opposite her mother and waited for them to explain.

Oh, my they're NOT getting married. Are they? Gros.

"You have a special visitor arriving tomorrow night to meet you. His name is Mr. Edward Anglophone," Martha said.

"I have? But…who he is?"

"Let me finish explaining. I know you must get going soon for work. This shouldn't take long."

Ribby nodded and Martha continued.

"When we were at the waterfront, we stayed in a lovely little B&B and met Edward. His friends call him Teddy. He owns his own library out there. We met him and got along. He invited us for drinks. He mentioned his library, his need for a new head librarian."

"He knew about you Ribby," John admitted.

"Me?"

"He knows people at libraries all over the world," Martha added. "And librarians."

"He keeps his finger on the pulse, since he's looking to hire a new one himself," John said.

"Yes," Martha added. "His library closed. That's why he wants to meet you."

"To take over his library?"

"Potentially," John said.

"Head Librarian? Me?" Ribby exclaimed. "I'm not qualified to be Head Librarian. You need a degree for that!"

We could totally be Head Librarian.

"Well, all I know Rib, is if someone owns their own Library, they can hire whoever they want to be Head Librarian. It's small Rib, not like the Toronto Library—but it's the opportunity of a lifetime. So, he'll be here at 8. You need to buy something new to wear. Gussy yourself up to make a good impression." Martha sipped her coffee. "Not to mention, he's completely loaded."

Now, she's hooking us, out?

Surely not.

Sounds like it to me.

"Yes, he has shed loads of cash. And no family. No relatives either," John said.

"I don't want to meet him. My job is fine. Besides, I don't want to move far away. I like it here."

We don't want to be pimped out! You, stupid old bat!

"Sorry Mom, but this opportunity isn't for me."

"Daughter, you're going to meet him and that is that!"

"Just meet him," John said. "What have you got to lose?"

Ribby pushed back the chair. Angela turned toward the stairs.

"When hell freezes over," Angela said.

Martha's chair scraped against the floor.

Ribby ran up the stairs and locked the door.

Angela threw open Ribby's closet and grabbed the wrapped knife. She waited.

If that bitch tries to get into this room, she'll regret it.

Footsteps. Stomp Stomp. Stomp Stomp. Two sets. Running. Laughing.

Ribby held her breath.

Minutes later, it was quite clear what they were up to. Martha cried, "Yes!" as the headboard pounded against the wall.

Absolutely disgusting.

Let's get out of here!

Chapter Twenty-Three

THE LIBRARY WAS IN chaos when Ribby arrived.

Mrs. P. Wilkinson, Head Librarian had been planning a Book Signing for months. It was her baby, since she was personal friends with Best Selling Children's Author P.K. Schmidlap.

As Ribby moved toward the entrance, two children shouted, "Hey, where do you think you're going, lady? We've been here for hours. You can't butt in!"

"I work here," she said flashing her Library Staff badge.

Once inside, she went to find Mrs. Wilkinson.

"It's mayhem out there," Ribby exclaimed. "Where is Mrs. Wilkinson?"

"Her husband called. She's in the hospital with a burst appendix. We don't know her password, so can't get the schedule from her computer. We expected a few hundred kids—not thousands!" Monica said with her voice trembling, "I don't know what to do. P.K. is only here for another sixty minutes because he has other commitments." She broke into tears.

"Oh my, you should have called me. Don't worry, I'll talk to P.K. and see if we can sort something out."

"You can't get past his minder, or rather, his wife," Monica said. "Over there—tall, blonde and full of herself."

Mrs. Schmidlap wore an expensive designer suit and six-inch heels. She looked at her watch several times as Ribby made her way toward her.

"Excuse me, Mrs. Schmidlap?"

"Yeeeeeeeees."

"Might I have a word with you? We have a problem."

"WE don't have da problem! YOU have da problem!" Mrs. Schmidlap shouted, causing her husband to drop his pen and the children to jump.

Tension built up all around Ribby.

"Eet is okay my darvlings," Mrs. Schmidlap said, taking hold of Ribby's left arm and pulling her aside. "You people are not organized. My husband, he signs for one more hour and then, zip, ve are gone. Ze children must not be disappointed, but he cannot stay. He has other commitments. Ve have other commitments," she whispered in an angry voice.

Ribby had to find a solution. There were at least 1,000 kids outside and another 50-100 inside. She had to convince P.K. to sign the books for the children who had been waiting the longest. He could do it if he sped it up.

"What about ze compromise?" Mrs. Schmidlap asked.

"Yes, good idea."

"We need to go at ze 12, on ze dot, no ifs ands or buts. We, P.K., cannot sign for everybody, not today. What if, zeeze childrens buy a copy of ze book today, or order it ve shall say today? P.K. will sign all orders and zey will be delivered here by the end of ze week, would that work?"

"All we can do is try. Thanks for the suggestion. I'll see what I can do."

Ribby returned outside. She pulled the door closed behind her.

"Hey, what are you doing, lady? We haven't seen P.K. yet! P.K.! P.K.! P.K.!" they shouted, surging forward.

"Stop talking everyone! Please be quiet and I'll explain!"

The children quietened.

"Okay, that's better!" Ribby said. She noticed the police had arrived as a precaution. "P.K. must leave here at precisely twelve noon to fulfill a prior commitment."

The crowd booed and jeered. The police moved in.

"P.K. will sign all of your books. We have your orders here. If there are any changes to our information, please let us know in writing before 5 p.m. today. You can pick them up here next week," Ribby suggested.

"In a week!? Everyone will already have finished reading their copies. They'll tell us the ending. They'll ruin it for us."

"You can take your book today and read it unsigned or leave it here for P.K. to sign, it's up to you."

There was some grumbling, and Ribby knew it could go either way.

Mrs. Schmidlap came outside to help and whispered a suggestion in her ear.

Ribby conveyed her message to the children. "If you leave your book today to be signed, you'll receive a free exclusive gift from P.K.—a limited edition—bookmark!"

The children cheered. Ribby and Mrs. Schmidlap embraced. The policemen tipped their hats. At twelve noon on the dot P.K. left in a limousine.

When it was all over, Ribby relaxed her shoulders as the tension melted away. The rest of the day thank goodness was uneventful.

On the way to their apartment, Ribby thought about the elusive Mr. Anglophone.

Maybe I should just see him?

Being Head Librarian would be cool and after today, you deserve it.

Yes, taking charge today made me feel like I could do it. I mean, be Head Librarian and when am I ever going to get another chance?

He must be really loaded, to have his own library.

Yes. But why me? He could ask anyone.

Never thought I'd say this, but Martha must be responsible for his interest.

Not to mention to consider me, for the role.

So, agreed. We will meet him.

Yes, agreed.

Chapter Twenty-Four

It was 8:34 p.m. on the following night when Ribby arrived home. She was wearing her black dress and shoes with high heels.

A limousine was parked at the curb.

The driver tipped his hat. "Nice evening," he said.

"Yes, it sure is beautiful," Ribby replied.

"So are you," the driver said with a wink.

This caught Ribby off guard.

Angela winked back.

Ribby huffed inside, but soon put on a smile when she entered the living room. "Good evening," she said.

Anglophone stood and reached out to kiss her hand. He was around 4 ft. 9 inches tall and about eighty years of age. He stood with a cane and wore an expensive tailored, blue-striped suit, with a red cravat.

"Would anyone like a drink?" Martha asked.

"I'd like," Mr. Anglophone said, "to take Ribby for a ride in my car. That is, if it's all right with her?" He glanced in her direction then looked at his watch. "We have reservations at the Revolving Restaurant for 9."

"I do apologize for being late."

Oh my god! He's probably not even going to make it through dinner! He's absolutely and completely geriatric!

"Oh yes, I understand beauty takes time," Anglophone said as he stood and extended his arm to Ribby.

Ribby took it.

Ribby and Anglophone made their way toward the door.

"Don't worry about getting her home early, Teddy. We know you'll look after her."

Oh my God! We are definitely NOT going home with THAT.

Ribby glared at her mother over her shoulder as they approached the car. Once inside Anglophone said, "Driver, you may go to our destination. I expect you looked on the map to see where it is?"

"Yes, Mr. Anglophone, Sir, the GPS is all set."

"Good, good. Then you are learning," Mr. Anglophone said. "Now close the partition so the lady and I can have some privacy."

Dirty old sod.

The limousine driver's eyes made contact with Ribby's in the rear-view mirror as he pushed a button. A glass partition rose between them. Red velvet curtains floated across, making the backseat into a private room. Mr. Anglophone pushed a button to reveal a bar with chilled Champagne.

"Ribby, my dear, I've been looking forward to meeting you."

Ribby, not knowing what else to say said, "Thank you, Mr. Anglophone."

"You may call me Teddy, as my name is Edward. Tell me though, where did you get your name, Ribby? Is it short for something? It is a rather unique, but lovely name."

Ribby laughed. "Strange. No one has ever asked me that before."

"If it's a secret you don't want to share, I completely understand, my dear."

He's an old smoothie. A charmer. I'll give him that!

"When I was a little girl, I couldn't pronounce my first name. It's spelled like Rebecca but pronounced Reee-becca. You know, with that terribly exaggerated long 'e.' I always pronounced it as Rib-ecca," She laughed. "Ma didn't like to shorten it to *Becky*. She thought it sounded too common, so she started calling me Ribby. It stuck, and it's been my name ever since."

"Well then, I will call you Rebecca if you wish, but I do prefer to give you a special name."

"The name I love is Angela. Would you like to call me Angela?"

OMG! Why are you doing this to me?

"Angela," Teddy said as it rolled off his tongue. "Very well then, Angela it is." Teddy brushed his hand over Ribby's knee.

Ribby decided the brushing had been an accident.

Angela wasn't so sure.

***

At the restaurant, the driver opened the door for Teddy first and then for Ribby.

"We'll be at least two hours," Teddy said. "I'll text you when we're ready to go."

"Yes, Sir."

"He's a damn fool most of the time," Anglophone said referring to his driver, "but loyal as they come."

Chapter Twenty-Five

There was a queue at the restaurant, but Anglophone's presence parted the way.

Like a gentleman, he offered Ribby his arm, and escorted her through the busy restaurant.

It was like an out of body experience for her. Guests turned their heads, greeted them, even raised glasses in a toast to them. She felt like a celebrity.

The couple continued to a Private Room. The ceiling was high, with a sparkling chandelier suspended from above their table. The table itself was set with beautiful plates, cutlery, and sparkling crystal flutes. A bottle of Champagne was chilling in a stand.

Once they were seated, Anglophone ordered for both of them.

Ribby felt like Bella in the Grand Ballroom in Beauty and the Beast.

He's old, but he's no beast.

Shhh.

Anglophone spoke about his businesses and his money quite a bit.

Ribby asked if he had ever been married.

"I nearly married twice. The women weren't who they seemed to be. Gold diggers, you know." He paused and moved closer to Ribby. "I had them both killed."

"You what?" Ribby said, almost spilling her glass of Champagne.

"A little joke, to see if you were listening," Teddy said. He laughed and patted the back of her hand. "Not many would fancy an old coot like me these days!"

Ribby had another sip of champagne. She was already feeling lightheaded.

"Right then. Let's find that lazy, no good driver of mine."

"I'm getting very tired," Ribby said. "Would you mind taking me home?"

"Of course, I mind, Ribby, I mean, dear Angela. The night is young, and we haven't discussed the role in my library yet."

"I've enjoyed this evening, but I don't think I'm qualified to take on the position. I am flattered, but..."

"Nonsense! It's not for you to decide! I have a good feeling about you and that's enough."

When they were back inside the limousine, Ribby asked Teddy to explain his last statement.

"I have money. Money makes it easy to have eyes everywhere. I know about you. For example, how you help your mother with her mortgage and how you also rent out a waterfront apartment."

Ribby gasped.

He continued, "How you selflessly entertain the poor sick children and how you single-handedly averted a stampede at P.K.'s book signing. His wife, Mrs. Schmidlap doesn't like many people, but she liked you. If you can work with her, you can do anything. The job is yours if you want it."

Ribby's head was spinning as Teddy pushed the button for the intercom and told the driver to return to her home.

He's been following us himself or he hired someone to do it.

"I still need to think about it."

"So be it then. You have seven days to decide. Here's my business card; you can reach me anytime day or night." After a pause, he said, "Wait a minute! Why don't you come up and see the Library for yourself? No time like the present. We could drive back together right now!"

"Uh, I don't know."

He offered you the job as Head Librarian. It's yours for the taking. I know he seems creepy right now, but he is telling us straight up. He's not hiding anything or lying about it. That's something. He's our ticket out. We can observe him, see what he's really like without making a commitment. Come on Ribby, take a chance. Besides, the driver is super cute. Look at those blond curls spilling out from under his cap.

Not to mention his blue eyes.

I know. I know. Besides, it could be fun!

"We'd be there by early morning. You can stay at the same B&B Martha and John holidayed in. Everything will be prepared for your arrival. It will help you to decide."

"But I don't have any other clothes—other than what I'm wearing."

"Ah, don't worry about that."

Ribby opened her mouth.

He anticipated her next objection. "I'll call your mother and explain."

Ribby wasn't sure about anything anymore. She went back and forth in her mind. Should I, or shouldn't I?

"It would be my pleasure," Angela said, taking Teddy's hand into hers.

You were taking too long to decide.

Ribby who'd been distracted by the driver looking at her in the review mirror cringed.

Teddy ordered the driver to take them home.

Ribby pretended to sleep on the way back.

Angela hoped Teddy would take a nap, so she could go up and sit with the chauffeur.

Teddy pulled out his laptop and began typing.

The over-zealous clicking is doing my head in.

I'm sure we'll be there soon.

Seconds later, *Are we there yet?*

Chapter Twenty-Six

THEY ARRIVED AT PORT Dover in the wee hours of the morning.

The driver opened the door for Teddy. "Take Miss Angela to Mrs. Pomfrere's. Don't come back until she's been introduced."

"Yes, Mr. Anglophone."

"Ask Mrs. Pomfrere to see to it that Miss Angela is up and ready for breakfast in four hours. Let her know you'll be there promptly to collect Miss Ribby."

"Yes, Sir," the driver answered, he got back into the car and drove away.

Ribby who had nodded off, now opened her eyes. She looked out the window, trying to see what Anglophone's house was like, but it was too dark.

A few moments later they arrived at the B&B. Mrs. Pomfrere rushed out to greet them. The driver made the introductions, then discreetly filled her in about breakfast at the Anglophone estate, and departed.

"I'm incredibly pleased to meet you, Miss Angela. Mr. Anglophone told me so much about you."

Ribby couldn't help but notice Mrs. Pomfrere's attire. Although it was exceedingly early in the morning, she wore an evening gown. "Thank you, Mrs. Pomfrere. If you're in a hurry to go somewhere, please don't let me hold you up. Point me in the direction of my room and I'm sure I'll be able to manage."

"Manage? Manage? Why I'm dressed this way to greet you. Now, please follow me and we'll get you all settled in!" They went inside, where she moved like a whirlwind along the corridor and up the stairs towards Ribby's room.

"You're even more sweet than I imagined. Teddy is surely smitten with you, and I can see why. My oh my, those legs of yours do go on forever, don't they?" Mrs. Pomfrere said in an overly familiar tone.

"Uh, well," Ribby stammered.

"This is your room," Mrs. Pomfrere opened a door.

Roses of all kinds and colours filled the room. It smelled heavenly. The closet door stood wide-open, overflowing with designer clothes.

"I do hope the sizes are correct. Teddy estimated. You'll find everything you need. Should you require anything else, I'm at your service twenty-four hours a day."

"You mean, all this is for me?"

"Oh yes, yes, the clothes and so much more. You're a lucky girl, you are. Having Mr. Anglophone on your side. He can do anything. He's like magic."

"Uh, yes I am," Ribby said, followed by a weak, "Thank you," as Mrs. Pomfrere closed the door behind her.

Wow! He's some kind of a guy.

He did this for me.

I guess that's why he was clicking away on his laptop for the entire trip.

Ribby suddenly laughed. She felt like a child in a candy store. Now that she had a second wind, she raced from one side of the room to the other, finding trinkets and gifts in every corner. In the bathroom was a Spa bath, filled with bubbles, awaiting her arrival.

She placed her elbow beneath the bubbles, and then broke the surface of the water. A delighted moan escaped from her throat. The temperature was perfect. She took off her clothes and lowered herself in. Bubbles tingled on her skin. She reclined, taking in a deep breath, and closing her eyes. She opened them again, to make sure she wasn't dreaming. She felt like Sleeping Beauty and she'd awoken to discover she was in paradise!

I could get to like this.

Me too!

Relaxed and in a comfy night dress, she snuggled down under the covers and drifted off to sleep.

***

"A<small>RE YOU AWAKE</small>, M<small>ISS</small> Angela?" Mrs. Pomfrere asked through the closed door. Without giving Ribby time to respond, the person knocked again.

Another voice, whispering. Teddy's.

Ribby covered herself, expecting them to burst right in.

"Well, get the key and wake her up!" Teddy demanded. "We have places to go and things to see."

Let me in! Let me in! Dirty old sod.

"You should've awakened her when the make-up artist arrived," Teddy exclaimed.

Make-up artist. Interesting...

"I did try, Mr. Anglophone, but she was sleeping so soundly, I hated to disturb her."

"I'll be out in five minutes, Teddy."

"I'll be waiting at my home for you. My driver will bring you to me when you're ready. Please don't keep me waiting."

Cool. Free time with the driver.

We have five minutes to get ready.

She took a quick shower, perused the chest of drawers, and discovered an array of silk underthings.

The old coot has remarkable taste.

And his eyes are fairly good too. These sizes are spot on!

He'd have a coronary if we walked out wearing only the silkies. I bet the driver's eyes would pop right out of his head, too.

Don't be disgusting. Ribby buttoned her silk blouse and zipped up her skirt.

Then came another firmer knock. "Excuse me, I'm here to do Madame's makeup."

He thinks of everything.

A small woman, around Martha's age, completed Ribby's makeup in a jiffy.

"I am Angela!" Ribby said as she beamed a smile at her reflection.

"Of course, you are," the woman replied nonchalantly.

No, you're definitely not.

Jealous?

"Thank you. I would offer you a tip, but I have no money on me."

"Oh, you don't need to tip me; Mr. Anglophone has it covered."

Ribby's stomach grumbled as she stepped into her shoes with spikey heels.

On the way to the limo, she walked like a drunk. The driver smiled when she nearly toppled over. If he liked her, he didn't show it. He opened the door for her without speaking.

The drive to the house was pleasant enough. Mrs. Pomfere's B&B stood in the centre of a small village. As the car meandered along the country road, Ribby caught a glimpse of Lake Erie.

"The Marina and the Lighthouse are over there," the driver explained. "In the winter, the Polar Bear Plunge is very popular."

"Oh, I do remember seeing something about that on the news. Since they take the plunge for charity, I admire the courage it must take." She shivered.

"My friend participated last year, he almost froze his," he paused, "his, uh, tackle off."

Ribby laughed.

He thinks you're too prim and proper to say balls in front of you.

Well, I am the guest of his boss.

"We'll be there soon," the chauffeur said.

They went through a few hamlets, small enough to notice but gone in the blink of an eye.

"We're here," the driver said.

Ribby sat up straight. Now that she was arriving at the main house, she wanted to take everything in.

Angela hummed the theme music to the television show *Dallas.*

The driveway leading up to Anglophone's home was overlong. Trees lined the boulevard, bending at the will of the wind. She shivered.

She craned her neck, trying to get a glimpse of the house. When she did, she breathed in and held it. It was not a beautiful house. With its narrow windows and dark brick edifice it felt cold, unwelcoming. A total contrast to the other house in which she'd stayed overnight.

It's downright Bronte-ish.
Look though, rose bushes.
Let's hope it's nice inside.
I'm sure it will be.

The driver stopped the car and came around to open the door. Ribby shivered as she stumbled across the tarmac.

Before she could knock on the front door, a man opened it. He was tall, thin wiry, and dressed from head to toe in black. He wore an expression one would have after sucking on a lemon.

"Hello," Ribby said.

With a high-pitched voice, he said, "Madame, Mr. Anglophone awaits your presence. You've kept him waiting for too long!"

"I'm sorry."

Don't apologize, he's the help. Push by—like you own the joint. You are Theodore Anglophone's guest. You deserve to be here.

Which is exactly what she did.

The gob-smacked man was not pleased, but he was a professional. He announced Ribby's arrival.

Teddy stood immediately, and with a flourish of his hand he said, "Welcome to my home."

Ribby scrutinized the room in which Teddy stood. Although he wasn't a tall man, in these surroundings he seemed tall. Even the coat of armor across the room was shorter than he was.

Knights were a lot smaller than I imagined.

Ribby smiled. "Thank you, Teddy. What an amazing room!"

Jackpot!

"My dear," Teddy said, "You look like a picture in it. In fact, I must have your portrait painted as you are now."

Teddy seems to have forgotten he was pissed off at us.

Ribby blushed. "Thank you so much—for everything."

"It's my pleasure, dear Angela. Now come here and sit across from me so I can watch you with the morning light coming in behind you." Teddy snapped his fingers and his manservant pulled out the chair for Ribby. "I trust everything was satisfactory at the B&B?"

"Yes, it's wonderful, Mr., uh, Teddy."

"I wasn't sure what you liked for breakfast, so I had my chef prepare two of everything." Again, he snapped his fingers, and the parade of food began.

"Oh my!" she said. Wafts of bacon, maple syrup, blueberry muffins and sausages reached her nostrils.

Talk about a smorgasbord! Enough food to feed an army!

The manservant directed his underlings to serve Mr. Anglophone first.

Anglophone clapped his hands.

The staff went straight over to serve Ribby. Anglophone clapped his hands again. "Tibbles, we must have Mimosas!"

Immediately a waiter cut two oranges in half and squeezed out the juice. Another waiter popped open a bottle of Champagne. The first waiter combined the two beverages. Ribby watched closely as the waiter poured each substance with great precision.

He handed a full glass to Teddy to test. Teddy nodded it was satisfactory. He filled a second glass and handed it to Ribby. They toasted to a pleasant stay and tucked into the food.

"I hope you don't mind, but I paid off your mother's mortgage."

Ribby gaped.

Teddy motioned for more coffee and it was poured. As he stirred, he added, "I also purchased the building your apartment is in."

Ribby gasped. She used the napkin to wipe the corners of her mouth.

That's an unexpected turn of events.

"Of course, you don't need to pay rent anymore. Save the money if you don't move here. Travel. See the world!"

Say something, anything.

"Oh, and I also paid off your credit card." He sipped his Mimosa.

"Uh, thank you. Very much. That's very kind of you."

Ribby felt uncomfortable after Teddy's announcements and it showed.

"Tell me, Angela, what is your heart's desire?"

"My heart's desire?" Ribby said, blushing. "I don't know."

"You must know what you want. A smart girl like you. Something always too far away from your grasp, and yet your heart desired it. Think on it. I shall ask you again in due time."

Ribby listened as Teddy spoke of his travels around the world.

"We could sit here and talk longer, but I'm very anxious to show you the library."

"Oh, yes. I can't wait to see it," Ribby said. The Mimosa had gone straight to her head. "But I'd like to get a little fresh air. I'm not used to Champagne this early. Is it too far to walk?"

Teddy laughed. "Not for a young sprite like you, it isn't, but you're wearing those inappropriate shoes." He snapped his fingers. A woman entered. "Please bring my guest a pair of suitable shoes." The woman bowed, left the room, and moments later returned with a pair of runners. "Change into these. I'll take your heels along with me in the car." Then to his manservant, "Tibbles, draw our guest a map."

"On the way, think on your heart's desire. Remember, I want you to name it."

The air was crisp and clean. It cleared her head.

He's so kind and gentle and giving.

He may not be what or who he pretends to be. Let's keep our guard up until we know what he wants. Remember nothing is free.

Ribby continued walking, her mind absorbed in finding an answer to his question.

Keep him guessing. Don't reveal our cards yet.

She rounded the corner; saw the limo and then the Library.

Stephen opened the door for Teddy who stepped out holding Ribby's shoes. She sat down in the limo and exchanged shoes leaving the flats in the back of the car.

"Here it is, my dear," Teddy said. The sign above the door read**: E. P. Anglophone: Private Library.** Under the sign was a plaque: Head Librarian: blank space.

I'm surprised our name isn't already up there. He seems quite sure of himself.

Behave.

"Come along," he said.

The large wooden arches welcomed her inside. Anglophone took her hand.

Ribby's heart skipped a beat. The library was round. Circular shelves. Books, books, and more books as far as the eye could see. Thousands and thousands. And ladders, at the ready, to take you to the top shelf. To the height of the ceiling, stained glass up some twenty feet high. When she looked up and turned around, she grew dizzy.

Teddy guided her to a chair which she fell into with a sigh.

"Satisfactory?"

"Oh, my, yes!" Ribby said, trying to harness her emotions. "It's like something out of a dream."

It's nice Ribby, but something doesn't seem right.
"Tell me now. What is your heart's desire?"
"This is it!"
What a little fool!
"Don't worry," Teddy said. "It can, and it shall, be yours. If you…"
Here Teddy stopped as his driver attracted his attention. "Uh, one moment please, Angela. Make yourself at home."
Ribby stood and wobbled. She climbed one ladder, came down and climbed another. Every author she could think of was here. Realizing the driver had returned and was standing below her, she adjusted her skirt.
"Oh, you scared me."
Not I! Come to me.
"I'm deeply sorry, but Mr. Anglophone has been called away. He asked me to escort you back to the estate when you're ready."
"I, I was…" Ribby said, stepping down without paying full attention. She mis-stepped and tumbled.
The driver, whose name she didn't even know, caught her.
Ribby flushed bright red. Their eyes connected. He put her down and walked away.
"Thank you."
He didn't respond.
He thinks I did that on purpose. That I fancy him.
Angela sniggered.

She followed him through the door and into the carpark, and then decided against taking the car.

"I prefer to walk," she said.

"Are you sure?" He glanced down at her shoes.

She raised her chin, and without responding started walking.

"Whatever Madam wishes."

You should have asked him for the runners.

I know! I know!

Back at the house with aching and blistered feet, Ribby spotted the driver sitting out front.

He tilted his hat in her direction, then covered his eyes and went back to sleep.

God, he's so cute.

Ha! Teddy would fire him if I mentioned he didn't give me my other shoes.

Don't you dare!

Ribby eventually removed her shoes and walked the rest of the way in her stockings.

The look Tibbles gave her when she entered the house with shoes in her hand was somewhere between a smirk and a grin.

To hell with him!

"Pardon me, Miss," Tibbles said. "Mr. Anglophone is detained. He'd like you to return to the B&B. I'll advise the driver to take you."

Well, I can't walk all the way there.

Nope, swallow your pride and get into the car.

There was an awkward silence all the way to Mrs. Pomfrere's which neither occupant was keen to break.

You're acting like a spoiled brat!
I don't care.
The car sped away and Ribby wobbled inside.

Chapter Twenty-Seven

R IBBY SLAMMED THE DOOR behind her when she returned to her suite. She tossed her shoes across the room, then flung herself onto the bed, muffling her sobs in the pillow.

He's oh-so-dreamy!

He knew I needed my shoes and yet, he didn't give them to me.

You didn't ask for them.

Still, he works for Teddy. I'm Teddy's guest. He should be trying to make me happy.

You're overreacting. Wash your face, it'll make you feel better and forget about it.

Problem is, I can't. I feel like such a fool. Me falling into his arms like, like, Jane Eyre.

Who cares? If he thought that, then he was probably flattered. Segue. The library.

It's beautiful, it's everything. But why does Teddy want me, an unqualified person to run his library?

See that's why I said you shouldn't put all your cards on the table. Now he knows that place is your heartfelt desire. He's playing Fairy Godfather and he has us by the tits.

My heart says he's on the level. That he doesn't have ulterior motives. But my head, oh my head.

Ribby grabbed her purse and pulled out the cigarette packet. She slipped one between her lips. Even without lighting it, the smell calmed her. Holding it against her lips she drifted off to sleep.

"We need to talk," Teddy whispered through the door.

Ribby sat up with the cigarette still hanging from her lips. She put it back into the packet. Speaking through the closed door she said, "Sorry, I must've fallen asleep."

"Get ready. I need to take you home now. Pack up your things and I'll meet you downstairs in the car."

She listened as he walked away then slumped to the floor, fighting back a sob.

Anglophone giveth and Anglophone taketh away.

But why? What did I do? Is this because of Stephen?

Don't be ridiculous.

No matter. It's all for the best. Change out of his clothes. Walk out of here with your head held high.

But the library. My heartfelt desire. Now that I've told him, he doesn't want me after all.

Ribby changed into the clothes she'd arrived in.

It's his loss, Rib. Remember, head high. Plus, everything we earn now, is ours. No rent, no mortgage, no credit card. We're basically debt free! Imagine how much fun we can have!

On the way out, she gave Mrs. Pomfrere a kiss on the cheek.

"We never say good-bye to our guests. We hope to see you again."

"Thank you."

The driver stood beside the door, waiting for Ribby. Once inside the car, she fastened her seatbelt. She turned her head and looked out the window, taking in everything she'd never see again and to masquerade her disappointment.

"Angela, this is strictly business. It has nothing to do with you or our arrangement."

"You mean you still want me?" Ribby asked with a shaky voice and her heart about to jump out of her chest.

"Of course, I want you to be my new Librarian," he said, brushing her thigh with his hand.

The perv. He's playing with you. Slap his hand away.

Ribby flushed. It was an accident. It was nothing.

The cheek of the old perv. I told you. Give him an inch...

"Driver, please put up the barrier. The lady and I would like some privacy."

Ribby looked up, caught the gaze of the driver in the rear-view mirror. Crossed her arms around herself.

Anglophone opened a bottle of water and handed it to Ribby requiring her to uncross her arms. She took it and sipped.

"Ribby, I mean Angela if the library is your heart's desire, then it is yours. What I have, is yours."

She sat upright, listening, but Anglophone fell silent. She took a few more sips of water, waiting.

Is he waiting for me to say something?

He's playing a game. Keep schtum. We put our cards on the table, let him do the same. Meanwhile, keep your cool. Enjoy the view.

It sure is pretty here, but my heart is racing.

Calm yourself. Take a few deep breaths. In. Out. In. Out.

Her breathing exercises were interrupted.

"What will you give me in return for your heart's desire?"

Here we go. Let me manage this.

"I, I have nothing to give you, Teddy. Only myself."

Seriously Rib, please shut the fuck up!

"Only yourself? You don't feel worthy?"

Ribby tried to speak, but the words caught in her throat.

He wants more Rib; he wants sex.

Ribby blushed beet red.

"Oh my, my," Teddy said, patting the back of her hand. "You look very worried, and I didn't mean to worry you. I'm an old man. I've lived without love, without touch, for an awfully long time. I could never expect you to love someone like me. Even if it was for your heart's desire."

"I," Ribby said.

"Shhh, let me finish. I wish to have you in my life. For companionship. Friendship. If you fell in love with me—if you could love me, that would be my heart's desire. Perhaps one day you will fulfill it."

Wow that was a curveball. Reverse psychology? Be careful.

There was silence in the car now and two extremely uncomfortable passengers. Ribby took a few more sips of water and Anglophone checked his phone.

"Will you marry me?" he blurted.

OMG that second curveball was so far out, I'm speechless, Rib.

Me too, I mean, what am I supposed to say. I want the library, but I don't love him.

We're young and vibrant. He's well, so far over-the-hill he's nearly down the other side. Wait, now...

Oh no, you're not thinking what I think you're thinking?

Means to an end. He wants you to be his friend, to run his library. He's not asking for sex, but for companionship and love. Right? So, if you are fulfilling his heart's desire and he is fulfilling yours, then, where's the harm?

Then why propose marriage? Even I know that it wouldn't be a legal marriage unless it was consummated. Just the thought of me and him...

I know, I know.

✱✱✱

Teddy occupied himself with his phone.

Ribby and Angela debated the issues at hand.

He's drumming his fingers again. So annoying! Now, he's clicking his pen-click clack, click clack, click.

He's waiting for an answer.

I don't know how I can accept. Give me one reason why I should say yes. How can I say yes?

Easy. One word: library. Two more words: Head Librarian.

Head Librarian of what though? I have no staff, no co-workers and at the moment no patrons.

But you'll be the boss of the books.

You're not helping.

I'm trying!

I know, but to him our relationship is nothing more than a business deal. We'd be man and wife, but only in name. I want a man I can love, who will love me in return. This is settling.

Settling? You call this settling? You're thirty-five-years-old and thirty-six is around the corner. You have no prospects, no future. This will give you a future. Teddy can open the world for you, for us. Love is not all it's cracked up to be. If you don't agree, you'll regret it for the rest of your life.

Ribby glanced in Teddy's direction.

Say something. Anything.

"I just need time, Teddy, to think about it."

Teddy stared into the distance.

Soon, but not soon enough the driver pulled to the curb in front of Martha's house.

***

In the darkness of the back seat, Ribby clenched and unclenched her fists. The rapid movement, the opening and the closing brought her to a decision. "Teddy, I'm certain we can come to a suitable arrangement."

Teddy threw his arms around her, beaming a smile. "Oh, thank you for making me the happiest old man in the world."

Well done, Rib! Bravo! Work with him. Work it out. Remember, we're in control here.

Ribby's voice trembled, but she managed a slight smile as she broke out of his embrace. "You'll need to give me a few days to tie up loose ends."

"I can wait for you Angela, but please don't make me wait too long. For you, I have already waited a lifetime," Teddy said as he kissed her hand.

Oh my, he is smitten!

They exchanged kisses on the cheek.

The driver opened Ribby's door, and he held it while she stepped onto the sidewalk.

"I'll call you in twenty-four hours," Teddy said.

Ribby nodded. Behind her on the porch Martha shouted, "Is that you, Ribby? Oh, hello Teddy." She waved.

Teddy waved back as the driver shut the door and returned to the front of the car. They departed.

"Yes Ma, it's me."

"You're back sooner than I thought you would be. Come inside and tell me all about it."

Ribby tripped her way up the porch stairs.

Chapter Twenty-Eight

RIBBY SAID HELLO TO Scamp with a pat on the head and the trio went into the kitchen.

"Ribby, sit down. I have a million questions for you. How did it go?" Martha babbled, not letting Ribby get a word in edgewise. "A cuppa, yes, I'll make you a cup of coffee and then...My, you do look exhausted."

"Ma, yes I am tired. It's a long drive. Mr. Anglophone, Teddy, is interesting."

"I thought you two would hit it off. Did he pop the question?"

She knew he was going to pop the question? She knew? What the?

"You knew he was going to?"

Is this part of some master plan? Oh now, this is deeply unsettling.

"He loves the library, and he wouldn't let just anyone run it."

Ha, ha, oh she means the library. My BAD.

"Of course not. He's very generous to offer me this opportunity."

"Mr. Anglophone made sure—before he even met you—-that you were the one."

What's that supposed to mean? Are we back to the Master Plan concept?

Ribby held back her fury. "You knew?"

Mommy Dearest stoops lower than low again.

"Now Rib, don't get your knickers in a twist. He meant well. He wanted to be certain. With all that money, he has to be incredibly careful."

Ribby sat quietly, stirring her cup of coffee.

Martha stood and busied herself by tidying up. She glanced at Ribby. "You're exhausted, would you like me to run a bath for you?"

Run a bath for you? Okay, take off your mask. Who is this woman?

"That would be lovely."

Later, in the bath, Ribby fell asleep and dreamed.

She was floating, stark naked, inside a pink bubble in Anglophone's library.

Anglophone came into view. He strutted around, red-faced and with clenched fists while his chauffeur shadowed him.

Anglophone said, "I want those new books to replace the old books immediately. Put them at eye level, so my girl can find them."

"This is not in my job description," the driver replied then turned his back.

Anglophone grabbed him by the arm, pulled him down and slapped him on the cheek. Although the slap was hard, the driver had been prepared for it and he didn't even flinch.

"Your job is whatever I tell you it is, boy!"

"Mr. Anglophone, I will of course do whatever it is that you want me to do, for her sake and her sake alone. I am yours to do with as you will," the driver said.

Anglophone let go of his arm. The driver straightened his back.

What hold does Anglophone have on him?

This is a dream. We're dreaming. Wake up, Ribby! Wake up!

Shhh, this is interesting. Try to zoom in on the books he wants us to see.

I'm trying, but...damn.

"I'm generous with you Stephen, and generous with her. I don't ask much of you. I'm an old man. I'm your employer. Do not be impertinent in the future."

"I apologize," Stephen said, bowing all the way to the floor with his hat in hand. "I can assure you it won't happen again. I expect this will take me most of the day."

"Very well. Then start refiling the books. Inform Tibbles when you've completed the task."

"What should I do with the old books?" Stephen queried.

"There are empty boxes in the back. Store them for now," Teddy said. "They mean nothing. We may give them away in future. For now, put them out of the way."

Teddy exited.

Stephen continued working. He glanced over his shoulder where Ribby sat naked in her imaginary bubble.

"Stephen," she whispered.

This is one weird dream.

Teddy is really hard on him.

Yes, he expects perfection.

Then what's he doing with me?

"Wake up, Ribby!"

Ribby's bubble burst as Martha came into the room.

"I've been knocking for ages."

"Sorry Ma, I fell asleep."

"Good. That means you're relaxing. Here's something to sip on."

Ribby hid most of herself under the bubbles.

"It's not like I haven't seen it all before, daughter." Martha laughed.

Ribby shivered then reached for the glass of Champagne. Martha sat on the edge of the tub.

"To you," Martha said as they clicked glasses.

This is way weird. This woman can't be your Mom. She's buttering you up like she knows the old guy popped the question and she's intending to move in with the two of you.

The soapsuds dripped down Ribby's arm and onto the stem of the glass. "Mother, how did you meet Mr. Anglophone?"

"I already told you this didn't I?"

"I don't think so. If you did, I don't remember."

"Well, we were at dinner, and Anglophone came in," Martha recalled. "He was very boisterous and demanding with the staff and seemed to be of some importance. We were curious who could cause such a scene. When I first saw him, he looked familiar. We thought he was a political figure, or we'd seen him on television. He seemed agitated and was abusing his limousine driver who was trailing behind him. Everyone stared at him."

"Did he notice?" Ribby asked. "I mean, that everyone in the restaurant was staring?"

"He had total disregard for the other patrons at first. When he realized he was causing a scene he apologized to us, not his employee. Then he bought everyone Champagne."

He sounds like a bully.

Agreed. "And that was it?" Ribby said.

"No, no my girl. After that, we asked him to join us, and he accepted. He treated, and we ate and ate. It was a wonderful evening. He invited us to stay with Mrs. Pomfrere as his guest. That's why we extended our holiday because it wasn't costing us anything."

"But then, how did I come into the conversation?"

"Over dinner, I'm not sure what we were talking about, but I told him about you. About your role at the library and volunteering with the children at the hospital. Teddy was well intrigued. He wanted to meet you. He mentioned his library. Said it was closed, until he found the right person to run it. He asked about you."

Do tell us more about stalker Teddy.

"He's very coy about it all, seeing he already knew about me."

"Knowing about someone isn't the same as getting to know them, daughter."

"Yes, but it sounds like he already decided."

"I don't know about that."

"He, Teddy, did ask me to run his Library Ma, but there were other conditions. Complications."

"Complications such as?"

"Such as I have to quit my job. Move somewhere new. I have to leave the children."

"Someone else will take over. You need to be selfish for once in your life."

Ribby relaxed a little and had another sip of Champagne.

"From what I saw of Mr. Anglophone he was very generous. Not a penny pincher."

I wonder if she knows about the mortgage.

It's not my place to tell her.

"True." Ribby shivered. "I need to think more about this Ma, and to get out of here before my body turns into a prune."

Martha stood and took Ribby's Champagne glass. "Daughter, you'll probably never get a chance like this again. I know I haven't always been the best of mothers. I know you'll make the right decision."

"Thanks," Ribby said. Once the door was closed, she got out of the tub, dried herself, and put her nightgown on.

That was absolutely and completely 'gag me with a spoon' mother and daughter time.

Mom was trying hard to be supportive.

Yes, she sure was. I could see the dollar signs in her eyes. But let's change the subject. Let's discuss that weird dream.

Yes, in my dream his name was Stephen.

I always thought he reminded me of Stephen Moyer from True Blood.

I haven't seen that series, but I know who you mean.

It was weird though, Anglophone replacing books with new ones. I don't get it.

Out with the old and in with the new. That's dual purpose. New books with a new Librarian. It makes perfect sense to me.

It felt more like a premonition.

Ribby laughed. I'm not clever enough to have premonitions.

But I am.

You are so funny.

Chapter Twenty-Nine

AFTER A HASTY MORNING, since she overslept, Ribby arrived at work and made her way into the building.

Immediately a banner reading: "CONGRATULATIONS RIBBY!" caught her attention.

Ro-ro. It looks like someone let the cat out of the bag. Who? Ma? I'll...I'll....

An avalanche of shouts and applause.

Oh no, I've got to get out of here!

No, you don't. It's too late for that. They see you. Smile!

Ribby smiled as her fellow employees gathered around.

"Way to go Ribby!"

"We knew you could do it!"

"We're immensely proud of you! Head Librarian! Wow!"

On the bulletin board was the following note: *"Congratulations to our own Ribby Balustrade! Head Librarian, E. P. Anglophone Private Library. Signed, Mrs. P. Wilkinson, Head Librarian."*

Ribby rubbed her eyes in disbelief. Opening them again, she mumbled under her breath. How could he have gone ahead and announced this without asking her first? She balled up her fists as heat rose in her cheeks. She was no longer in control of her life, her destiny. She went behind the counter and put her head down on her desk.

Snap out of it, Rib. You're spoiling their joy. They're so proud of you and it's your last day here. Take it in stride. Hold your head high.

But he promised! He said I could take the time. Now this is my last day. MY LAST DAY!

What's done is done. You can tell him off about it later. For now, enjoy the moment. Be an inspiration.

Mrs. Wilkinson wandered over to the desk. "First, I want to thank you for covering for me when I was in the hospital. Second, I'm so proud of you, Ribby! When Mr. Anglophone called me, I mean *the* Theodore Anglophone, I felt so proud of you. I cried. I really did. You've always been like a daughter to me."

"Thank you, Mrs. Wilkinson."

"I mean, such a powerful man. For him to choose you, at your age, to be Head Librarian. You're going places."

"You've heard of Mr. Anglophone before?"

"I don't know him personally, but I know OF him. Besides that, the architecture of his library was in several magazines. As was his home."

"Yes, the library is quite beautiful, so is his home, but I didn't know about the magazines."

"We're having a luncheon in your honour. Full catering, thanks to Mr. Anglophone, who insisted on covering all expenses."

"Oh, he did, did he?" Ribby said.

That crafty old beggar.

"In the meantime," she continued, "enjoy your last day."

"Thank you, Mrs. Wilkinson."

Ribby glanced in the direction of her co-workers who had returned to their tasks. Curious, she logged into the computer and *Googled* Theodore Anglophone.

The most searched item was a newspaper article in the local paper. The headline read: "Suspicious Death in Local Library."

What the?

Ribby read on.

The Head Librarian died?

That's why he closed it. Sounds like the woman was crazy.

Oh, Teddy found her body. That must've been awful for him.

No, look here. It says he called the police, but the reporters arrived first.

Reporters always arrive first. Oh, they have photos of the woman. She looks insane. Where are her clothes? And she looks like she's spitting at the reporters.

Many would like to spit at reporters.

Agreed, but look at her eyes. She looks desperate. Fearful.

Hysterical. It says Teddy closed the library after that, swore he'd never open it again.

Until now. I need to get out of here for some fresh air before this luncheon begins. She approached Mrs. Wilkinson and asked permission to go.

"Well, I can hardly fire you now, can I?" Mrs. Wilkinson roared. "After all, this is your last day!"

"Yes, oh true," Ribby said. More well-wishers cheered when she walked by. Once outside, she pulled a cigarette out of her bag and lit it up.

Perhaps, we've been a little hasty.

A little!

***

Ribby returned to the Library in time for the luncheon. The array of food in the buffet was more than enough for all. Everyone munched, mingled, and chatted.

Mrs. Wilkinson began singing, "For she's a jolly good fellow." Ribby's cheeks grew hot. Mrs. Wilkinson made a short speech, then presented Ribby with a gift.

"Open it! Open it!" her colleagues sang out.

She tore the package open. It was a cellphone.

"We already added all of our contact details so we can keep in touch," Mrs. Wilkinson said.

As if we'd want to keep in touch with this lot!

"Thank you, very much," Ribby said.

"Speech! Speech!" they called out.

Ribby was unaccustomed to public speaking and mumbled out a few incoherent sentences.

I'm getting verklempt.

She said she'd miss them all.

You've done it, Rib. Now, let's get the heck out of here.

They applauded. Mrs. Wilkinson drew everyone's attention by clearing her throat. "I'm giving Ribby the

rest of the day off! Thank you Ribby, for years of outstanding service with the Toronto Library. Please keep in touch."
   The staff formed a procession.
   It's like a wedding.
   Or a funeral.
   Outside a limousine was waiting at the curbside.
   Ribby clenched her fists.
   Whoa, take a deep breath.
   The driver got out.
   Stephen.
   He tipped his hat, then proceeded to open the back door. Inside Teddy was waiting with a huge grin on his face. He patted the seat, encouraging Ribby to enter.
   Get in and cool down first before you say anything.
   Right. She unclenched her fists. Sat down and fastened her seatbelt. She took in a deep breath. "Hello, Teddy."
   "Close the door, Stephen!" Teddy barked.
   Stephen. His name really is Stephen.
   Kind of Twilight Zone-ish isn't it?
   "Onwards," Anglophone ordered. The barrier went up and the driver drove on.
   "I hope you've had a pleasant day, Angela."
   "It has been rather strange," Ribby said. "It was my last day after all." She took a deep breath. "I didn't know you were going to inform Mrs. Wilkinson of our arrangement. I wanted to resign myself. It was an important thing for me to do." Her cheeks flushed,

and her voice trembled as she fought to maintain composure.

"Why should you do what I can do for you?" Teddy whispered. He placed his hand on her leg.

This time there was no doubt about his intentions. He left it there. She did not remove it.

"I know these people at the Library have not always been good to you. I know they have taken advantage of you, and they have not appreciated you. I want you to leave them. I want them to know that you are better than they are. You win and they lose."

What the? We knew he was watching us, but this is...extreme...

True. Wonder what else he knows?

Ribby took a deep breath.

"I know many, many things about you. About the world," Teddy confessed. "Snivelling fools are a dime a dozen. They aren't fit to lick your boots. If anyone has hurt you, point them out to me and I will deal with them."

And a hitman! Rib, this is totally heading in a wacko direction.

Ribby had been digging her nails into the door handle. She released it. "No, no, there is no one like that. I lead a quite simple life. I work, I go to the hospital, I come home, and I don't have much of a social life at all."

Keep calm. Maintain calm.

"You will." He lifted his hand open palmed, like he intended to give her a high five. She followed his hand as it rose, and as he put it down at his side again. "When we're together, the world will bow to you and everyone will love you and wish to please you."

The description of a Queen or Princess.

He looked into Ribby's eyes. Her stomach lurched. She kissed him.

Ah geez, Rib...wtf?

"I'm sorry," Ribby said, disgusted with her actions. *It's your fault. I saw myself as a Queen or Princess.*

Me too, but we were locked in an ivory tower.

"It was a lovely gesture," Teddy said. "And even better because you had the impulse to do it yourself and followed it. Yes, I see that we will be happy together. Come back with me now. Come to our home. Let us begin our lives together today."

"Wait, Teddy, wait. I still need to put some things in order."

"Let's dine together this evening. Let's celebrate!"

"I'm exhausted Teddy and I want to spend some time with the children at the hospital. I need to say good-bye and to tie up some loose ends."

Teddy glanced away for a second when she paused.

He knows.

Maybe, but I kissed him.

Yeah, you sure did. Why?

I honestly don't know.

Weird.

"Yes, I see that is something you must do. But I am drawn to you. I want to be near you. I want us to be together. Let me take you home, Angela," Teddy pleaded.

"Actually, I do appreciate the offer, but I'd prefer to catch the bus."

She touched the back of his hand.

"Where would you like us to drop you off?"

"Here, right here is fine."

Stephen stopped the car. Before he could get out and open the door, Ribby opened it and stepped out.

"Until we meet again," Teddy said, blowing a kiss in her direction and without breaking contact with her eyes.

Ribby found herself catching it and putting her fingers to her own lips.

Blech, Rib. You are going way too far.

It was like I was possessed or something.

That was an Academy Award winning performance. I mean, I have said some things and I have done some things but you, Ribby, you take the cake.

Bite me!

Chapter Thirty

RIBBY ARRIVED BACK HOME and heard her mother sobbing.
"What is the matter, Ma?"
"It's your Aunt Tizzy. She's dead."
"I don't believe it."
Good acting, Ribby.
"Yes, I couldn't believe it myself, but they found her body. She was in the Attics-R-Us van with one of my beaus."
"Oh."
"He was a strange man," Martha said.
You can say that again.
"That's awful. Poor Aunt Tizzy."
"I just returned from identifying her body. They're calling her husband and daughter now. They shouldn't see her, not if they can get out of it. They should remember her, how she was. Not as I saw her. All bloated and…." She went to the bar and poured herself a jig of whiskey neat. She downed it.
"How, how did it happen?"

Ribby, this is another Academy Award winning performance. Steady. Keep your voice steady.

"They think she drove off a cliff in his van after stabbing him, as he had a stab wound in his back. The forensic team called me in, they said she was raped."

"Raped? Oh, my goodness, how horrible."

"Wait a minute. Remember that knife I found the other day? Where's that knife? It could be a murder weapon. What did we do with it?" she said shaking Ribby. Then she stopped and went paler than pale. "And Mr. Anglophone...oh, this scandal could ruin everything for you!"

"What does he have to do with it?"

"I mean, about me. About my gentlemen callers. If it comes out, it'll ruin your chances."

Ribby slapped Martha hard.

Again. Again.

"You've got to get yourself together, Ma. None of this has a thing to do with you, with us, and Mr. Anglophone won't give a hoot about any of it. Besides, he is no stranger to scandal."

"You know then?" Martha asked.

"Yes, I know about the former Librarian who died in Anglophone's library. It all sounds very bizarre."

"The men," Martha said. "The men may tell, and their wives may tell, and everyone will know that your mother is a whore."

"Oh, please Mother, stop rambling. You're doing my head in."

"Promise me something, Ribby. Promise me you'll ring Teddy and tell him you want to join him now. Get yourself out of here and out of the city. Before the scandal hits."

"But Ma, the Anglophone estate isn't far from the city. Teddy would find out. I just left him. I have loose ends to tie up. I'm not ready to go yet."

"Noooooooooo!" Martha yelled. "You must get out of this house NOW!" Martha ran up the stairs and started throwing Ribby's things into a suitcase.

Ribby followed.

She's losing her mind, Rib.

I see. She's falling apart.

Martha continued packing folding and rolling her hand-me-downs. Mumbling to herself, "I'm saving you. You're all that matters."

Ribby, not knowing what else to do yelled, "STOP!"

Martha stood as still as a deer caught in headlights.

Ribby explained. "Mr. Anglophone has given me a wardrobe filled with amazing new clothes." She grabbed the bag she took with her on hospital performances and threw it over her shoulder.

You're not going to be needing that!

Maybe I will and maybe I won't but I'm not leaving it here.

"Oh, I see," Martha said, unpacking. "Call him back. He can't be far away. Daughter, if ever you loved me. If ever you could forgive me and do this for yourself, then please do it NOW!"

I think you should, Rib.

Agreed. When I'm gone, she'll pull herself together. *The state she's in, I don't know.*
She has to.
Ribby called Teddy.
"Sure thing, I'm not far away. I'll come and collect you."
Martha and Ribby hugged.

As the limousine drove away, Martha watched her daughter until she could see her no more. She closed the front door and dropped to her knees. She remained there for a second or two with her back resting against the door.

Martha's life flashed before her eyes, everything good she had done and everything bad. There were more bad things, than good. Only Ribby fell into the latter column. She remembered her sister when they were close years ago. A sister who she'd fought with over nothing. A sister who she would never see again.

Her mind wandered back to the knife she found. How cagey her daughter had been about it and how she'd even made a joke about Tizzy killing someone with it. Strange. Not to mention how vague her daughter had been about her sister's return. It was all rather strange. Something wasn't right. She wondered where the knife was now. Her daughter was involved, of that there was no doubt.

She imagined what could have happened. Carl Wheeler might have showed up. Had Tizzy opened the blinds? If they were opened by accident, Carl would have walked in like an invited guest. And then, she gasped. She sat down, thinking about what could have happened. How her daughter could have walked in...what she may have seen...

She ran up the stairs to Ribby's room. Her daughter hid things in her closet, had done so since she was little. Sure enough, Martha found the knife wrapped in a towel. And not just the knife, but her daughter's bloody clothes.

She took the knife outside and buried it under the floor of the shed along with the bloody clothes.

She went back inside and poured herself another whiskey. This time a large one. The phone rang, but she didn't answer it. She just sat there, sipping, and sipping until it rang itself out.

Chapter Thirty-One

THE RIDE TO TEDDY'S house was a quiet one. In her peripheral vision she noticed Teddy had fallen asleep. Unable to sleep herself, she decided to give Martha a ring.

It rang several times with no answer. "Pick up Ma, pick up. I know you're there."

"Ah, um, what?" Teddy said, waking up startled.

"I'm sorry to wake you, Teddy. I'm trying to ring my mom."

"Oh, how is Martha then?"

"No answer," Ribby said, putting the phone back into her handbag.

"Never mind," Teddy said, patting Ribby on the thigh. "You can ring her in the morning. Can you tell me, Angela, what were you thinking about?"

"When?" Ribby asked.

"Before I fell asleep," Teddy remarked. "You seemed lost somewhere deep in your thoughts."

Ribby started to say something, but Teddy interrupted— "Angela, it's not a criticism of you, but when we're together, I would hope you would only be thinking of me. Of us."

Now he wants to control your thoughts.

I don't think that's what he means.

"Since I was a little girl, Ma had to raise me on her own."

"I know that, Angela. Martha told me. She said she was often a bad mother. And yet, you worry about her. How quaint." He took her hand into his.

Take out the violins.

He fell asleep again, holding her hand.

More nap time is good!

Chapter Thirty-Two

THE NEXT MORNING THERE was a disturbance outside Martha's house. Horns honking. Tires screeching. Cameras flashing. Loud voices.

Martha lifted the corner of the blind. It was mayhem. One woman carried a sign which read: "Get Out of Our Neighbourhood You Whore!"

"There she is!" someone shouted, as cameras clicked and flashed.

"She's home!"

Martha went into the kitchen and made a cuppa. As she sipped, Scamp sat close enough so she could pet him.

She called John MacGraw and left a message. "It's me. Don't come over today. Lie low for the next few weeks. Reporters, bastards, are crawling everywhere. I don't want you to be implicated. Call me when you can…" The message time ended with a beep. Martha put the phone back into place hoping he'd hear the message before his wife did.

She sat down, flicked through the TV channels until there was a knock on the door.

"Martha, it's me, Sophia."

Through the keyhole she spied her neighbour, Mrs. Engle.

"Stand back you, you vultures!" Sophia shouted with her fists in the air. "This woman is in the privacy of her own home. SHOO! You lowlifes! Go chase an ambulance or something!"

Martha opened the door. One reporter shouted, "Why was the Attics-R-Us guy here so often? They found his appointment book, and he visited you weekly."

"No comment," Martha said as she closed the door behind her neighbour.

Mrs. Engle slipped in. "Whew! I need a cuppa, Martha, my friend."

"You sure deserve one. I just made myself one. And thanks Sophia."

"It was nothing. I heard about your poor sister. Those vipers should leave you to grieve instead of creating a fuss about stuff and nonsense."

"I guess it's a slow news day," Martha said as she poured the coffee and offered Sophia sugar and milk.

Sophia waved both away. "Where's Ribby?"

"She's gone. Thank goodness. She has a new job, out of town."

"Good for Ribby. In the meantime, I'm sure another event will turn their attention away from you. Those vultures could learn a thing or two about manners!"

"They sure could," Martha said.

Sophia dialed 911.

Martha smiled as Sophia began to talk.

"Yes, is that the police?" She paused. "Well, you all better get on over here or I'm going to have to take the law into my own hands. Mhmmmm. Reporters everywhere. Tramping down my roses. Disturbing the peace. I don't know how they dare. Okay, yep, Sophia Engle, 44 Midas Lane. I'm trapped next door, 42 Midas Lane, okay. Will do. Okay. Thank you, Sir. See you then. Praise the Lord!"

Martha and Sophia waited for the police to arrive.

It didn't seem so bad now that she had someone with her.

Chapter Thirty-Three

It was midnight when the limousine pulled up in front of the Anglophone mansion. It was not entirely dark, and a light glow of something candle-like emanated from the windows.

The house opened its arms and Ribby stepped inside, followed by Stephen lugging her bag.

Teddy stopped at the doorway where his manservant stood.

The manservant assisted his master by removing his coat.

When he glanced at Ribby, a chill ran down her spine. He smiled, an unwelcoming smile. A smile still resembling someone who had been sucking on lemons.

It must be his usual state.

His puckered lips changed to a toothy smile when Anglophone faced him.

"This is your new home, Angela. Welcome!" Teddy said, beaming. "Stephen, drop the bag and you may go. The car needs a clean, both inside and out."

"Yes, Sir," Stephen said.

Stephen bowed first to Teddy and then to Ribby and left.

"This is my manservant, Tibbles. You met him the other day. He is responsible for running the house. Tibbles, Miss Angela. I trust all is in order?"

"Yes, Sir, everything is ready for your young lady's arrival," as he picked up Ribby's bag and walked away.

Ribby unsure what to do, looked at Teddy for guidance.

"It has been a long day, and I wish to retire, my dear," Teddy said, kissing her hand. "TIBBLES!" he bellowed. "Please show Miss Angela to her room."

Tibbles waited at the top of the stairs with Ribby's bag.

Ribby climbed the staircase toward Tibbles, "Aren't you coming up?"

Teddy remained at the bottom of the stairs like Rhett Butler watching Scarlett O'Hara.

"My quarters are on the ground floor. Good night, my angel. Sleep well."

When Anglophone was out of earshot, Tibbles huffed. "Follow me," he said, leading her along the corridor. A few doors down, he flung open the door and waived Ribby inside. He followed her in and waited for instruction.

Ribby took in her new accommodations. Her new home. Flowers filled every available space. Roses. Hundreds of them. Everything in the room was pink, pretty and beautiful.

"I trust this is satisfactory," Tibbles said. He dropped the bag onto the floor.

"Yes, oh my, yes." She turned and tipped over a bud vase which smashed to the floor. She dropped to her knees and started to pick up the pieces, all the while apologizing.

"I'll get that," Tibbles said, pushing her aside and pulling out a small broom and dustpan from inside his jacket. "If there isn't anything else, Miss Angela, might I retire for the evening?"

"Oh yes, thank you and, thank you very much. For everything."

Tibbles bowed and almost smiled.

Perhaps he has gas.

Ribby laughed.

Tibbles closed the door on his way out.

Once he'd gone, Ribby opened a door, which she hoped led to the bathroom. It was a walk-in closet. She opened another door; it was a powder room but no loo. Where then, was the bathroom?

"Tibbles?" Ribby called, but he had already gone. Guess I'll have to wait until morning.

Isn't there a bell or something you can ring to summon him back again?

I don't see one.

When you're Queen of the Manor, you'll get one installed.

Yes, it'll be top of my priority list.

Ribby shivered into her nightgown. She turned on the electric blanket and tried hard not to feel like a Princess who had to pee.

***

R IBBY WOKE UP IN the middle of the night with pains all along her sides. She had to get up and find the loo, and the sooner the better. Stepping onto the bearskin rug beside the bed, she shivered and searched for a cloak. She found one attached to a hook in the closet. It fit. Again, Teddy knew women's sizes.

He thinks of everything.

Yes, except for telling me where the loo is!

Poo-faced Tibbles should have done that.

Ribby opened the door and peered down the hall for the bathroom. Every step she took was painful.

That man should be fired.

No, it's my fault—I should have asked.

Ribby walked to the end of the hall. She started opening doors. Door number one was a guest room. Door number two was a boy's room all in blue.

What the...?

Maybe he has a son? And left his room as it was when he moved out?

Yes, some parents do make shrines to their kids.

At door number three, Ribby wrapped her fingers around the handle.

"May I, help you?"

Ribby turned, to find Tibbles, with his hand on his hip wearing a nightgown, a cap and carrying a candle. He looked like a character from a Charles Dickens novel.

"Uh, I'm sorry to disturb you, but I need to go to the loo. I don't know where it is."

Tibbles blanched. "Follow me." He led her back along the hallway, past her own door and, two doors down, to the right, to the bathroom. "Will there be anything else this evening, Miss?"

"No, no, Tibbles. Thank you very much," Ribby said as she rushed inside and made her way toward the loo. Peeing had never felt so good before, and she noticed the acoustics in the room were very loud. She had the urge to say something to see if it would echo back—but decided not to.

Angela though could not resist and began singing the chorus of Madonna's "Like A Virgin." *These acoustics are awesome!*

After she completed her ablutions, she looked around the bathroom.

Wow, towels with "Angela" embroidered on them.
How could he have arranged that?
The manservant probably sews.
He seems very...
Stiff? Stodgy?
Yes, and yes.

Anglophone certainly thinks of everything, I mean, eerily so.

Yes, he is thoughtful.

That's not what I meant. Never mind.

Ribby returned to her room and went back to sleep.

Angela was getting bored with Ribby's take on everything. She wanted some excitement; she missed clubbing and everything that went with it.

Angela wondered about Stephen. Was he single? Did he like to have some fun?

She didn't want to ruin the gig with the old man, though.

When the timing is right, all of it will be mine!

Cue sinister laugh!

Chapter Thirty-Four

THE NEXT MORNING, RIBBY opened her eyes to the sound of someone knocking on her door. Before she could answer – this felt like déjà vu – the person knocked again.

""I'll be out shortly," she said, as she threw back the covers, stretched and yawned.

"Master Anglophone awaits your presence, Miss. He doesn't like to be kept waiting. Please hurry."

"I'll do my best," Ribby said, then the woman went away. Ribby showered, tied up her hair and fixed up her face by pinching her cheeks. She returned to her room, grabbing the first thing she could get her hands on from the wardrobe. It was a suede pantsuit which fit her perfectly. She went downstairs.

"Good morning, Teddy," Ribby said, as Tibbles led the way into the dining room.

"Finally!" a woman attendant muttered under her breath.

Tibbles glared at her with his eyes nearly popping out of his head, then at Anglophone. When he was certain Anglophone hadn't heard her, she was dismissed.

"Yes, well, Angela, do sit down and enjoy the first of many breakfasts we will share in this house as a couple. Did you sleep well? I understand Tibbles assisted you at 2 a.m.?" Teddy clapped his hands. The staff began serving.

"Uh, yes," Ribby said, going scarlet. She glanced over at Tibbles. He looked at his shoes.

"Tibbles has been reprimanded for neglecting his duties. It will not happen again."

"I do apologize, Miss Angela," Tibbles said, bowing low to Teddy and then to Angela.

"It wasn't his fault. I should've asked."

"I assure you it always is the fault of the help. When you are an employer, you should never need to ask."

Ribby focussed on her food. The server came to her side and offered to pour cream into the oatmeal. Ribby thanked her. "I don't believe we've met?" Ribby said to the server who stepped back and covered her face. Ribby looked in Teddy's direction. His upper lip trembled. She realised she'd blundered.

"Mrs. Haberdash, may I introduce you to Miss Angela," Teddy said in a sarcastic tone. "Now leave us to eat our breakfast in peace. I don't want the lot of you milling around in here. Bad for the digestion!"

"Sir?" Tibbles asked.

"Yes, I do mean you, too. I'll let you know if we need anything."

"Yes, Mr. Anglophone, Sir."

It's all so formal in here, it gives me the creeps.
Yes. They seem frightened.
Teddy runs a tight ship.
Tibbles is scarier.
Anglophone must pay them well.
Ribby looked up, realizing Teddy had been speaking.
"...Don't be afraid to make suggestions for the future, so you can make the library your own."
"Teddy, before you say anything else, I want to thank you."
Teddy beamed and puffed up his chest.
"You, my angel, are everything and more. I want to give you what is mine. Anything you wish, I will give you. All you need to do is ask."
Ribby stood and kissed Teddy on the top of his head. She hugged him. He encouraged her to sit upon his knee. They kissed. Gazed into each other's eyes.
Get a room! I mean, the servants might come back any minute!
Teddy stood and placed his hands on Ribby's cheeks. He stared into her eyes, and she into his. He led her away by the hand.
Totally barfing here.
Along the corridor, into the heart of the entrance way, up the stairs.
Snap out of it, Rib! It's too soon to get carried away.
No reply.
Ribby, are you listening to me? He's hypnotised you —or he's controlling you. Ribby! Listen to me. Come back to me!

Angela attempted to take control. To look away. To break the bond was all she needed to do, but she was unable to.

She shouted Ribby's name again and again and again.

Still, no reply.

Chapter Thirty-Five

THE HEADLINES SCREAMED, "A Whorehouse in Our Midst." Martha grabbed the newspaper on her doorstep and tossed it straight into the trash.

She pulled it out again and against her better judgement read the article. 'Martha Balustrade, 62, operated a brothel near downtown. (Photo on Page 3).'

Martha flipped to the photo. She gasped. They had used her wedding photo. She felt betrayed. A tear trickled down her cheek as she tore the paper into tiny bits.

Martha felt every inch of hollow space, like her house was no longer her home. She had taken the phone off the hook and refused to turn on the television for fear of what was being said about her. She wished she'd never climbed out of bed, but she needed to go up into the attic.

She climbed the ladder. Far back in the corner, buried under blankets, cobwebs, and miscellaneous paraphernalia was a padlocked chest of drawers which contained private documents.

Martha began removing papers from the chest one by one, stopping every now and then to read. There it was. She opened the book and unfolded the document inside: Ribby's birth certificate. She closed the book and turned it over. For a few seconds she looked at the image on the back. She refolded the document and placed it back inside the book and added it to the 'discard' pile.

When night fell, Martha climbed down, carrying as much as she could. She went up again and filled her arms, being careful to keep two separate piles. After several trips up and down the stairs, she had all of the documents with her. She intended to read the 'keep' pile more thoroughly with a whiskey or two. The other pile would be destroyed.

She placed the 'discard' pile on the couch near the fireplace and the 'keep' pile at the far end.

On the top of the discard pile was the book containing Ribby's birth certificate. She glanced at it briefly. At the blank space where the name of Ribby's father should have been.

Martha moved toward the fireplace and set the logs alight. She tossed in Ribby's birth certificate, then opened the flue. The wind whisked down immediately causing the papers on the couch to shiver and shake. She picked up the book and tossed it into the fire. She watched it set alight, then threw in the rest of the 'discard' pile.

When the lot was gone, Martha watched the rising sun cresting over the hills. The green lawn contrasted with the purplish red of the sunrise. Her eyes wandered to a small shadow cast in front of the door. She couldn't see anyone and wondered what it was.

She went to the door and peered out the peephole. She was certain it was a bottle of something. Milk? No, the milkman hadn't been around this area in a decade or more. In the end, her curiosity got the better of her and she opened the door. It was a bottle of sparkling wine, with a note saying, 'A Toast to You, All My Love.'

It had to be from John. He must've dropped by when she was in the attic. She picked up the phone to thank him but just got his answering machine. She hung up this time without leaving a message.

Martha poured a glass, downing a few sleeping pills at the same time. She continued with the wine and the pills until both bottles were empty. Then she went back to the Jack Daniels and polished it off.

She drifted in and out of sleep.

A spark in the fireplace connected with the edge of the 'keep' pile. Soon the pile was on fire. Then the sofa.

Martha slept on.

Mrs. Engel called the fire department.

Martha had taken care to keep the piles separate. In the end, both ended up in the same place.

Chapter Thirty-Six

TEDDY LED ANGELA ALONG the corridor.
Ribby, what are you doing? It's too soon. Are you asleep? Wake up! Wake up!
Teddy stopped walking and flung a door open.
Now, THAT is not what I expected.
Nor me!
Finally, you've snapped out of it! You really had me worried there.
Why? What happened? What did I miss?
You didn't hear me calling you?
No, but I could hear the ocean.
He must've done something to you.
I don't think so.
She stumbled forward, expecting to see a lavish boudoir, when in fact what was before her was nothing of the sort. In his home, he had created an exact replica of the library.
"It's for you," Teddy said, as he kissed Ribby's hand. He stood watching her as she took it all in. "This is your shrine, your special place, Angela, and no one will have the key except for you. Come here to quiet your

thoughts. To escape from the world. From me if you wish to. Come here to write, to paint, whatever your heart desires. Come here often. Get to know every book—read everything—for I have already read them all—and we will have much to discuss. One day, we will travel and see all the places you read about in these books. I want to show you everything."

Ribby rushed over and kissed him. No one had ever been so thoughtful, so wonderful, to her before.

Slow down, Ribby. Slow down!

He took her face into his hands and kissed her passionately.

Ribby's knees buckled.

Tibbles cleared his throat. "Excuse me, Sir."

Thank God for Tibbles! Ribby has left the building. Snap out of it, Rib.

"What is it?" Teddy said, with a stomp of his foot.

"A matter of great importance, Sir." Tibbles' voice trembled. He kept his eyes lowered to the floor.

"Not now, Tibbles. Keep it under your hat, old man, I will be out shortly," Teddy said, caressing Ribby's back.

"But Sir…"

"Very well then," Teddy shouted as he dropped his hands to his sides and left Ribby standing alone.

Ribby felt hot, safe, and happy as she looked around at the books in her own library. She pinched herself to check she wasn't dreaming.

I don't get it. Why have an exact replica of the other library here?

It's very thoughtful, don't you think?

I think it means he wants you here, not there.

I can't be Head Librarian here. There are no patrons. She shivered.

Yes, none of it makes any sense.

The other library had a good feeling about it. It seems cold in here.

There's a thermostat on the wall, perhaps it's cooler because some of the books are fragile, maybe even ancient? Look at that shelf over there. The bindings look authentic. Wait a minute, I just realised...is this the library from the dream?

An unexpected knock on the door made her jump. She got up and opened it to find Tibbles with a grave look on his face.

"My master had to leave the house on urgent business. He will not return until tomorrow. We are at your disposal." He bowed low.

"I'm fine for now, thank you, Tibbles." She closed the door and returned to reading.

Chapter Thirty-Seven

"WHEN DID YOU LAST see her?" Anglophone barked as Stephen drove away from the mansion.

"Friday. I was there on Friday. She was distraught, but I never thought she would do this!" Stephen said, digging his fingers into the steering wheel.

"She's a foolish woman," Anglophone said as his fist came crashing down upon the armrest.

The last thing Stephen wanted was to talk to him at all. But he had no choice since 'Teddy' was footing the bills for the hospital his mother was in. Stephen's mother had changed forever one day at Anglophone's library. She almost died. Now, she was a shell of the mother he had once known.

As he drove, Stephen remembered his mother telling him how she and Teddy's future became entwined. Although he had entered Anglophone's home as a babe, Stephen was never treated like family. Sure, he had a nice room with everything in blue, but a boy needed more.

Stephen had been a lonely child. A child who longed for a father figure. Anglophone closed himself off to his stepson. In fact, he left the room whenever Stephen entered. Stephen felt like a thorn in the man's side and nothing more.

   He wiped a tear from his cheek as he drove ever closer to the psychiatric hospital. Nurse Beemer told him his mother had swallowed a bottle of pills. When he asked where she got them, they weren't sure. It didn't matter. What mattered was his mother was unconscious. Her stomach pumped. Her future was more uncertain than ever. Would she live or die?

   "Stupid woman," Anglophone mumbled. "Stupid, stupid woman."

***

After Stephen opened the door for Anglophone, he ran ahead. He wanted to find his mother; he needed to find her immediately. He could hear Old Lead-foot swaggering along behind him. He never could understand how his mother could have fallen in love with him. But now wasn't the time.

Stephen approached the nurse. "My mother? Where is she? How is she?"

"She's out of danger, but it was a close call, Mr. Franklin. Room 208. Down the hall, to the left." The nurse released the buzzer.

Stephen went inside. He was determined to speak to his mother alone. He broke into a sprint.

Anglophone nipped at his heels.

His mother lay unconscious, embraced by the bedlinen. Tubing and wires extended from her chest and arms, leading to an array of machines.

Stephen kissed her on the forehead, sat down and took her limp hand into his. The machines hummed and beeped.

"She looks well considering," Anglophone said from behind Stephen's left shoulder.

"Now, get up, and let an old man have the chair. And get me a cup of coffee," he added, tossing Stephen a few bills. "And some flowers for your mother, nice ones, in a vase."

Stephen did as he was told.

One thing being around Anglophone every day for so many years did to a man, was to make him learn how to hold his tongue.

***

"Rosemary, can you hear me?" Teddy whispered to the woman on the bed. "Rosemary, it's Teddy."

There was no change or movement from the woman. Teddy remembered the day they first met. She'd been so vibrant, so alive. Only a few weeks ago, she'd celebrated her birthday. He'd sent her daffodils, her favourites.

Thankfully, Rosemary said she didn't remember much of anything from the time of the accident. News of her death hit the web. During the media mayhem, Anglophone had his friend, the coroner, send a car to whisk her away. Away to this place, where she was able to heal over time.

"She isn't really alive now, like this," Teddy mumbled to himself as footsteps approached. Stephen was returning. Teddy hadn't even spoken to his wife yet. For yes, since she was not dead—Teddy was still a married man. Half of everything he owned belonged to the unconscious woman and his heir.

"How is she?" Stephen knelt by his mother's bed and took her hand into his once again.

"She's breathing, but not by choice. It's about time we talked about letting her go in peace."

"But you can't. She's my mother, and I won't let you."

"Keep your voice down. You, impertinent imbecile!" Teddy shouted.

Rosemary opened her eyes. She opened her mouth.

"She's trying to talk!" Tears streamed down Stephen's cheeks. "Mother, I'm here, it's Stephen. Your son Stephen. If you can hear me, squeeze my hand."

He waited, holding his breath but she never squeezed his hand.

Instead, she squeezed Teddy's hand.

Chapter Thirty-Eight

BACK AT THE HOUSE, Ribby was feeling lonely. She wanted to visit the library but had no key. She considered asking Tibbles if he had a copy somewhere—but decided against it.

Ribby picked up the telephone in the entryway, planning to call Martha.

Tibbles appeared out of nowhere. "May I help you, Miss?"

"Yes. I'd like to call my mother and I seem to have misplaced my cell phone."

"No phone calls are to be made during your settling in period, Miss."

"But why?"

Are we being held prisoner?

"I'm following my master's instructions. Now, if there isn't anything else…"

"Well, there is something else. I'd like a key to the Library down the road, so I can go and have another look."

"There is no key for your use, Miss. You may go for a walk or partake of the facilities in the household, such as your own personal library. The spa is relaxing if you would like me to show you where it is."

"No, thank you. I'll wait for Teddy, er, Mr. Anglophone to return."

"I was coming to see you about Mr. Anglophone. He has been detained another day. I have instructions to make sure you feel at home. Let me know if there is anything more, Miss."

"In that case, I'm going for a walk. How far is the nearest village?"

Tibbles stepped closer to Ribby, leaned in and whispered. "It's too far to walk, Miss, and I'm afraid the car and driver are with Mr. Anglophone. Explore the garden area, let us know when you would like to dine." He walked away.

"Thank you," Ribby muttered. She turned and fought the urge to kick something. Instead, she walked out the door.

I miss Mom.

We're better off without that witch anyway! Look at the place we're living in, and if we play our cards right, we can make something of ourselves here. Although he's a little strange, Teddy is very fond of you. All you have to do is play along, until we figure out what his game is.

What do you mean his game? He wants me to be his companion. He's extremely sweet. I could fall in love with him. If you stopped making insinuations. Why are you so suspicious?

It's a gut feeling. Like he's done this kind of thing before.

He's so sweet and tender.

He cares for you. Still, after what happened before he showed you the library replica, you know, when you were out of it? Be on your guard. Tame him. Make him go slow. Keep him waiting. Guessing.

His touch is quite gentle.

After she explored for a while, Ribby looked ahead of her, and there was nothing but water. Behind her, Teddy's house. Then nothing for miles and miles.

She'd been thinking about some ideas for things she'd like to introduce to the library. Like a Kids Club. A place kids could go on a Saturday morning. To hear stories read to them, to play games. It would be a safe space, where parents could take a break. Yes, that was her best idea yet! She also wanted to talk to Teddy about resuming her performances at the local hospital. She missed—all her kids and wondered how they were doing. Her life had changed so much, and she felt somewhat overwhelmed by it.

It's only the beginning, Ribby thought as the mist from the waves kissed her face.

A car pulled into the boulevard and sped right past her.

I wonder who that is?

It was a woman.

Yes. Visiting Tibbles when his boss is away. Interesting.

It might be nothing, then again. If he's up to something, Teddy would want to know about it.

It would be fun to find out.

Let's go!

Chapter Thirty-Nine

ALL HELL HAD BROKEN loose. After Stephen's Mom had squeezed Teddy's hand, he had squeezed back. He thought he was doing so discreetly until the patient said, "Teddy, stop it god damn it, you are hurting me!"

"Mom, oh, Mom, you're awake. I better get someone in here." He pushed the button on the intercom. "Nurse, Nurse, come to room 208! Please!" Stephen wiped his tears away and kissed his mother upon both of her cheeks.

"Stop slobbering all over me, boy," Stephen's Mom said, looking him over. "I don't know who you are. Teddy, tell him to go away so we can be alone together. Get him out of here!"

Her denial cut through him. "But, Mom, it's me, Stephen, your son." He touched her hand, dropped something into it. "You gave me this St. Christopher's locket. See? It has your name on it, Mom. Read it."

She looked at the piece of jewelry and read aloud, "To Stephen with love from Mom. Hmmfff. Well, I don't remember you. Get him out of here, Teddy!"

Stephen left fighting back the urge to pound his fists against the hospital walls.

Chapter Forty

RIBBY RACED UP THE steps.

She opened the doors. A large backside of a woman wearing a long, sunflower print skirt came into view. The garment brushed the floor as she walked along behind Tibbles. A big floppy hat, and a long-sleeved, jade blouse with flowing cuffs completed her ensemble. Although she was behind Tibbles, she seemed to be leading the conversation.

Let's get out of here. She looks more boring than Tibbles.

No, Teddy told me to make myself at home. So, introducing myself, not to mention checking and welcoming newcomers would be appropriate.

That's Tibbles' job.

Ribby decided to interrupt; to attract their attention, she shouted, "Hello!"

The two turned in her direction, Tibbles with a cross look and the woman's mouth open since she was in mid-sentence.

Ribby hurried to where they stood gawking. Extending her hand to the new guest she said, "My name is Angela. And you are?"

The woman closed her mouth and looked in Tibbles' direction.

"Ah, Miss Angela. You have returned," Tibbles said. "I trust you enjoyed your walk?" He didn't wait for an answer nor did he attempt to introduce the two women. "Lunch is served in the Library. I am under strict orders from Mr. Anglophone to see to his guests. Enjoy your lunch. Should you require anything else, do let us know."

Tibbles with his hand on the woman's back, led her along the corridor and into his office. The door clicked shut.

Hmpft! He's such a bossy know it all.

Why would we want to spend time with her anyway? She looked like she might be able to turn anyone into stone! Or bore them to death.

You're probably right.

Let's see what's on the menu for lunch.

She made her way to the library. She lifted the silver lid, and found a lobster sandwich, loaded with mayonnaise. A bottle of Champagne was chilling.

Ribby tucked into her food, examining books while she ate. One volume caught her eye. "Sorcery Through the Dark Ages." Ribby picked it up.

Whoa, did you feel that?

I sure did. It, breathed. Ribby turned the pages. It's filled with Black Magic. Spells and incantations. The pages are very fragile. Most of the pictures are hand drawn.

I think the paper is made from skin.

Not human skin?

I can't say yes for certain yes, but it's possible. The ink on the pages might be blood.

Human blood? Ewwww.

I think you should put it back.

I've seen lots of old books before, but none like this one. It makes my hands tremble. Besides, it's just a book. What could be the harm?

It gives me the creeps.

Chapter Forty-One

"I'M HERE FOR YOU, my dear Rose," Teddy whispered, holding her hand.

"Cut the bullshit," Rosemary said. "My lad is out of earshot."

Teddy laughed. "Ah, glad to have you back. Please continue."

"First things first, Teddy," Rosemary said. She leaned in closer to him. "I want out of here, today, tomorrow—soon. I complied with your wishes, for our son's sake. I let them drug me, put me under—do everything except for a lobotomy—to keep my son safe and well, and now the time has come. Stephen is a man now, and he needs to know who his father is, and why we never told him."

"Rose, our agreement is that our son receives fifty-percent of everything. On one condition. The condition is, he never finds out I am his biological father," Teddy said. His voice ended with a gruffness almost like a bark. "You agreed after the incident at the library to go away. To let me get on with my life—in peace—so long as your son, our son, would be provided for. I have kept to my end of the bargain and you...you have no choice but to keep to yours. Otherwise, my offer will be rescinded. It's in my will. If he finds out—he will get nothing. NOTHING!"

A nurse passing outside the room said. "Shhhhhhhh."

"Oh, sorry," Teddy said.

Rosemary whispered, "I agreed, but cannot live here, in this hospital...this prison. Being watched twenty-four-seven—like a caged animal. I want our son to have what he deserves, but it kills me every time I tell him I don't know who he is. It hurts for a mother to see her child in pain."

Anglophone handed her his handkerchief.

She continued, "It's the only way I can talk to you alone. To keep on with this ruse and I'm tired of it. I want a life of my own. Otherwise, bury me here and now so he doesn't have to come to me anymore. I can't bear it! I can't bear to live like this anymore." Rosemary raised her hands to cover her face.

"So, that's why you swallowed those pills, to rid the world of yourself! Too bad you weren't successful. Too bad."

"Yes, it is too bad. I would have been happy never to see you again."

Anglophone stood. "I'm going now and leaving you to it." He turned his back on his former wife and lover and moved toward the door.

"If you go now, I will tell him. I *will* tell him."

"And make him lose everything?" He walked back to her bedside. "You will not tell him. You have sacrificed too much already." He hesitated, tapping his bony finger on his chin. "I will ask the nurse to take you out for a walk every day, so you can have some fresh air if that will help. And books. I can send you books. Make a list. My library is your library."

"Thank you, Teddy. Thank you. Yes, send me the latest novels. Magazines. Gossip. Even newspapers. They don't let us watch the news here...I don't even know what year it is."

"It is 2016. We will keep you on our chain here, but we will loosen the collar. See to it that you do not create another scene with a suicide attempt. I will keep my part of the bargain if you keep yours. For now, goodnight my Rose. I will not return. I will arrange to get you everything you need if you send a letter to Tibbles marked confidential."

"Thank you, Teddy. Thank you," Rosemary uttered. The swinging doors burped Teddy's exit and moments later Stephen's return.

"Are you okay, Mother?" Stephen asked, moving toward her bed.

"I am feeling somewhat better. Sorry to have scared you as I did. Of course, I know you. You are Stephen, my boy."

"If you didn't know me, ever again, I would..."

"Hush now. It was a drug induced lapse. I'm still recovering."

"Yes. You see things differently in the light of day?"

"I do, Stephen I do, and I am going to try harder to get well so I can get out of here. I'm going to start reading again. Maybe even writing again. One day they will let me out of here. You can show me your life."

"To get better Mother, you need to talk about what happened. All those years ago. At the library."

"Stephen. Stephen. Stephen. Stephen," Rosemary continued saying his name over and over again. Stephen shook her, but she was gone.

***

It was difficult for Stephen to concentrate later.

In his mind, his mother repeating his name replayed. *Stephen. Stephen. Stephen.* He always heard her saying that now. Every night. Every day.

Her calling his name and never knowing he tried to answer.

Chapter Forty-Two

RIBBY SAT CROSS-LEGGED ON the library floor. Another book caught her eye: *Everything You Ever Wanted to Know About Black Magic (But Were Afraid to Ask)*. She laughed at the title and at the silhouetted guy on the back cover.

What a dweeb.

Wonder what Anglophone is doing with these weird books?

He said this is my library.

Yes, that's weird too. Why he'd put them into your library.

There are lots of books here, it's not like he could have known which ones would stand out, make me want to look inside.

You were drawn to those two, immediately. Almost like they were lit up.

Ah, you're making too much of this. Just listen:

You, too, can become an expert on Hexing. All you need to do is persevere. First, choose a subject on whom you wish to place a Hex. Note: hexes are negative things. Do not put a hex on someone you love (unless it is a love/hate relationship or unless you get a kick out of seeing someone you care about in pain.)

Once you have chosen your subject, begin collecting their personal artifacts. The hair from a comb or brush, or pillow. Fingernails. Toenails. (Note: discarded ones please!) Rings. Watches. Don't be obvious about it. Remember to hide them in a safe location.

Special note: Practise in front of a mirror how you will respond when they ask, "Have you seen my watch?" Especially if you aren't a particularly good liar. Always have an answer prepared. An alibi. Be prepared to cast aspersions.

Ribby attempted to pour another glass of Champagne: the bottle was empty.

She inserted her index finger into the page where she'd left off. The house was quiet, almost too quiet for her liking. She stole up the stairs like a naughty child and climbed into bed fully clothed.

What a lightweight.

***

"WAKE UP, RIBBY. IT'S Stephen. Wake up."

Ribby covered herself, expecting to find Stephen, but he wasn't there.

It was a dream. Pity.

Her head pounded. The perspiration ran off her forehead, onto the cover of the book. On wobbly legs, she carried it down the hall to the bathroom. The stain had already set. She used a facecloth to blot it out.

She pulled out the blow dryer and zeroed in on the damp area. She returned to her room and put the book on top of the night table to dry.

Now that she no longer had anything to focus on the nausea rose and caused her to sway from side to side. She took a deep breath, trying to fight the need to retch but it didn't work. She ran down the hall, just making it in time. She felt a little better when she rinsed her mouth and brushed her teeth.

Since her head was still pounding, she returned to her room. She climbed back into bed and pulled the covers over her head.

Chapter Forty-Three

As he couldn't sleep in the motel suite, Anglophone obsessed about Angela. He had much to do, and time was ticking away. First, he had to announce her to the world, as his new librarian and as his intended wife. She was already under his spell, easy to compel and his need for her grew daily.

For years he'd searched for a suitable partner: an earth angel. His Angela fit the bill. Her selflessness with the children at the hospital, her naivete of men. Not to mention, she was without a doubt a thirty-five-year-old virgin. Practically unheard of in this day an age. A perfect candidate to study for his new book. And yet, after they wed, after...he wondered if she'd turn out to be just like all the rest.

He clicked on the television and spent the rest of the night binge watching reruns of *Supernatural*.

Chapter Forty-Four

THE NEXT MORNING, STEPHEN'S beeper buzzed. Mr. Anglophone was summoning him. Stephen ignored one beep, but then came two long beeps and finally three more beeps. He knew from experience letting Anglophone wait was ill-advised.

"Beeeeeeeeeeeeeeeeeep." Mr. Anglophone was losing his patience.

Stephen groaned. He couldn't afford to lose his job with everything else.

"Oh, all right," Stephen yelled as he closed his motel door behind him. He rounded the corner to find Anglophone waiting for him beside the limousine.

"Sir, sorry to keep you waiting, Sir," Stephen said.

"Hurry up, I couldn't sleep in this damned motel and I want to get home to sleep in my own bed. Come now. There is nothing more we can do for your mother."

Stephen opened the door for Anglophone. He waited for him to fasten his seatbelt, then returned to the driver's seat. He started the car and pulled away. He glanced at Anglophone in the rear-view mirror. "I called the hospital a few moments ago, Mother seems to be improving. They said she had a good night's sleep and ate some breakfast."

"She is in the finest of care," Teddy said.

"Thank you for—"

"You are very welcome, Stephen."

Chapter Forty-Five

WEEKS WENT BY WHICH soon turned into months. Anglophone was away most of the time. When he and Ribby were together, she asked for things, things which she thought would make her existence more fulfilling.

"I'd like to learn how to drive," she'd ask during dinner.

Anglophone would dab the corner of his mouth with a napkin. "But you already have a driver at your disposal."

"He's away with you most of the time," she pouted.

Don't ask him, tell him. Say we're bored out of our brains. Say we…

"Let me think about it," he'd reply. He never did.

During the day, Ribby spent most of her time at the library. She moved things around, reorganised them. But it was a quiet and lonely place. Something about being there, made her feel even more lonely. It was too quiet, and she longed for the soothing sounds of the water fountain in Toronto.

Ribby said nothing more about learning to drive. The next time he was back, she had other requests in mind.

"I'd like to order some things, for the library. I mean the main library," she'd ask.

"Whatever your heart desires," Anglophone would reply.

"I'll buy a computer, a laptop..."

"No need. You can use the computer in Tibbles' office." He took a sip of his coffee. "TIBBLES!" His manservant arrived. "Let Miss Angela use the computer in your office anytime she wishes to order things for the libraries."

"Yes, Sir," Tibbles replied. He glanced at Ribby, bowed, then left.

The following day, Ribby requested to use the computer and was ushered into Tibbles' office. He stood behind her the entire time and she found it difficult to concentrate let alone to order anything. In the end, she gave up on the idea.

At dinner on another occasion, "I'd like to book the car to take me to Simcoe Hospital so I can visit the sick children."

"It's such a small hospital, nothing like what you're used to. Besides, you have the library, and your responsibilities will increase as we get ready to launch the reopening," Anglophone replied.

I didn't want to go there anyway.

Sad when he was away and sad when he returned. Her new life wasn't all it was cracked up to be.

Chapter Forty-Six

TIBBLES WAS WAITING OUTSIDE on this occasion when Anglophone returned.

After Stephen left, Anglophone attempted to retire fully clothed.

"I'm full of beans, Tibbles."

"You certainly are, but why?"

"Oh, things are looking up. I'll fill you in later."

Tibbles insisted on removing his master's clothing. He replaced them with Anglophone's favourite red satin pajamas.

Once his master settled in under the covers, Tibbles set the music box in action. A chorus of *Lullaby and Goodnight* sang out from the apparatus.

Five winds should do it, he thought.

Tibbles picked up Anglophone's clothes and left the room. He looked at his watch. At his master's request, a new girl was starting in a few hours. He returned to his room.

Chapter Forty-Seven

RIBBY YAWNED AND STRETCHED. Above her on the ceiling, patterns of ghost-like figures walked in never-ending circles. She watched them with a sense of curiosity.

You feel at home here, relaxed, but you must keep your guard up. Be careful because Teddy isn't Prince Charming. He's more like Grandpa Charming.

That's rude and you're paranoid.

Ribby gave her armpits a sniff and then headed into the shower. Dressed and blow drying her hair, Ribby thought about Martha again.

How can you miss that old bag?

No matter what, she's still my mom.

You're too trusting! And sometimes you're a sentimental fool.

I feel like I should give her a call. She was certain things were going to hit the fan.

She knows where you are; if she needs you, she'll call.

Ribby returned to the room and looked out the window. She spotted Stephen beside the limo.

A knock at the door interrupted her thoughts. "Who is it?"

"Do you wish to have breakfast in your room this morning, Miss?"

"Is Mr. Anglophone still away?"

"He returned, but he's indisposed. Since you're dining alone, would you prefer to eat in the garden?"

Ribby opened the door to find a young girl with a friendly face. "That's a wonderful idea. You're new, aren't you? What's your name?"

"Yes, I am. I'm A-Abbey, Miss. My name is Abbey."

"Well, Abbey, I'm happy to make your acquaintance," Ribby paused as she heard someone approaching. It was Tibbles.

"May I be of assistance?"

"No thank you. Abbey has everything under control."

Tibbles glanced in Abbey's direction and the girl trembled. He then dismissed himself with a bow and disappeared around the corner.

"It's my first day. Thank you, Miss."

"Whatever for?" Ribby asked with a smile. "Since we're both rather new around here—we can learn together," as she invited the girl into her room.

"I'll get everything ready, Miss. In fifteen minutes?" Abbey curtsied. Her eyes smiled when Ribby spoke again.

"Yes, I'll be there soon," Ribby said, closing the door behind her. She invited Abbey to sit down and join her.

She's the help, Rib, don't be preposterous.

"But, Miss, I can't," the girl said, eyes moving side to side like she was expecting Tibbles to show up at any moment.

"Not even if it was an order?" Ribby said with a wink.

Are you trying to get this girl fired?

"Miss, it would be wrong. Tibbles is my superior," she whispered.

"I understand. What Tibbles doesn't know won't hurt him, right? Tomorrow, bring breakfast to my room if Mr. Anglophone isn't dining."

"It would be my pleasure," Abbey said relieved.

You don't ask the help to eat with you. Silly fool. I can't stand Tibbles either, but he is Anglophone's right-hand man.

I don't care.

All I'm saying is, Teddy dear is not going to like it.

I'll cross that bridge when I get to it.

Chapter Forty-Eight

After a few hours of sleep, Anglophone summoned Tibbles.

"A party! This evening. Here. Today. Caterers. Here's the guest list. Tell them they must attend...I mean everyone who is anyone. Courier or hand deliver the invitations immediately. My chauffeur is at your service. Call these top ten guests. They must attend. Understood?"

"Yes, it will be done. So, you have decided she is the one?"

"I've been waiting for the timing to be right, and tonight is the night. I feel it in my bones. It's time to tell all and sundry about the re-opening of the Library. We'll introduce our new Head Librarian, my fiancée at the same time."

"And Miss Angela, shall I inform her of your plans?"

"She is aware of my intention to announce her new position and our betrothal."

Tibbles fluffed the pillow and replaced it behind Anglophone's head.

"I want to surprise her with it all. Tell the fashion crew to be here at 5 p.m. ---no earlier and no later. The party will begin at 8 p.m., sharp. Those who are late will not be allowed entry. Ensure they understand PROMPT means PROMPT," Teddy said. "For now, I'm much too revved up but need to rest. Please leave me until 3 o'clock. At that time, prepare an Afternoon Tea for Miss Angela and I in the garden."

"Yes, Sir," Tibbles said with a bow. "Would you like me to wind the music box, to help you get back to sleep?"

"Of course, of course Tibbles. Thank you. Three turns should do the trick; after-all, it is only a nap."

After winding the music box, Tibbles bowed his way out of the room. He mumbled to himself as he checked the bannister for dust on the way down the stairs.

There wasn't any.

Tibbles sat in the foyer and went over the party details. He'd already arranged the caterer. Everything was coming together.

***

Sometime later, Anglophone was trying to sleep. His private line sounded. He waited for the answering machine to kick in. When it didn't, he got out of bed to answer it.

"Hello, Teddy," Martha said. "I know you said I should only call you on this line if it was an emergency."

"I'm listening."

"I need your help."

"How so?" Teddy asked.

"I'm in jail, accused of murdering my sister, and the man who raped her. I swear I didn't do it. I swear."

"I understand, but I don't know how I can help you. Do you need me to hire a lawyer?" Anglophone paced. Having his nap cut short made him cross.

"I'm calling you because I'm going down for this. I plead guilty and my lawyer says it won't be long until the judge sentences me."

"How can your predicament have anything to do with me? I am a busy man."

"Thirty-four-years-ago, you picked up a young girl. She was soaking wet. She was stranded on the road late at night."

"No, I'm not in the habit of picking up passengers in my limousine."

"You were driving. Oh, you don't remember. But I remember. It was me. You picked me up and together, we…You are Ribby's father."

Anglophone fell back onto his bed in disbelief. He wracked his brains, trying to remember. It was a trick. He knew it was a trick. "What kind of car was I driving?"

"It was a Mercedes Benz. Grey."

It was true.

"On that night, you saved my life in more ways than one. You must believe me. I need to know you'll look after her. She's your daughter. Will you do that for me? And will you promise me, you'll never tell her I'm in here?"

"I don't know what to say. I'm speechless." He paced. "Why admit to something you didn't do? Why prevent your own daughter from visiting you?"

"It's all I ask of you."

"Leave it with me. Let me think on it. If she's my daughter…"

"She is. Definitely." She paused. "And thank you."

Anglophone slammed down the phone.

That impertinent slut. How dare she do this to me?

Teddy could not sleep. His head was pounding. He was prone to migraines at certain times of the year and Martha's news had given him a doozy.

He rang for Tibbles.

Tibbles picked up on his master's condition immediately. "There, there," he said, "All will look better in a few hours." He offered a snifter of whiskey and a sleeping tablet. Anglophone downed it in one gulp then pushed the glass back to his manservant.

When Anglophone was calm and quieted, Tibbles wound up the music box and tidied up the room.

"Anything else, Sir?"

Anglophone was already fast asleep.

Tibbles smiled and closed the door behind him.

***

Tibbles double-checked his party to-do list while thinking about his newest employee, Abbey. He took notice earlier of the two young women whispering. That could be a good thing or a bad thing. He knew he wasn't popular and yet, his dedication to Anglophone had no boundaries.

Abbey had come, with high recommendations from a household in the city. A local girl he hoped would keep an eye on Miss Angela.

When he found her in the garden, he was curious and agitated. "Miss Angela how came you to be breakfasting in the garden today?"

"It was m-m-my idea," Abbey admitted interrupting him. "It is such a beautiful morning!"

Tibbles gave her a cross look and continued to address Ribby. "Afternoon Tea will also be in the garden. Mr. Anglophone wanted it to be a surprise—so please do act surprised. He will be joining you."

"Oh, pardon me. One can't dine outside enough when the weather is fine like today," Ribby said winking at Abbey.

"Very well then," Tibbles said as he excused himself.

"Whew! That was a close call," Abbey said wiping her brow.

"Don't you worry, Abbey; I can handle dear old Tibbles. Keep coming up with ideas. I'll put in a good word for you with Mr. Anglophone."

"Thank you, Ma'am," she said, unable to hide the thrill in her voice.

"None of that Miss or Ma'am stuff Abbey, not when we're alone. After all, we are friends."

"Friends," The two girls said in unison.

Gag me with a spoon.

Chapter Forty-Nine

Anglophone awoke from his nap and summoned Tibbles.

On a normal day, Anglophone pulled the summoning cord once. If it was an emergency, he pulled the cord twice. Today he pulled it three times.

Tibbles stumbled over his own feet as he threw himself along the corridor. He wished he could fly. In his arms, he carried all his plans and confirmations for the party of the season. Everything was perfect. He'd accomplished more than he'd set out to do. All the socialites' attendance was confirmed. He couldn't wait to fill Anglophone him in on the details.

Tibbles knocked, then poked his head inside. Anglophone was still in bed. The covers were pulled up to his neck and he wore a milky white complexion.

"Tibbles, I'm not well, not well at all. My head is spinning and I'm afraid…"

"Excuse me, Sir," Tibbles interrupted, "Might I get you some more tablets?"

"No, no, Tibbles. This isn't the kind of headache that is going away any time soon. I'll be out of business for the rest of the day. I want to be alone. In the dark."

"But this evening Sir," Tibbles protested. "The party."

"Cancel it."

"But..."

"I SAID C-A-N-C-E-L IT!"

"Very well, Sir," Tibbles said, biting back the anger in his throat as he bowed out of the room. He closed the door and departed.

Tibbles called Viveca Hartman at The Local Voice. He asked for her help in getting the word out.

"I'll do anything I can to help," Ms. Hartman said.

"Thank you,' Tibbles replied.

Chapter Fifty

VIVECA ENDED HER CALL with the notorious Theodore P. Anglophone's Manservant, Tibbles. She hurried to the office of the City Editor, Frank Munson, and told him the latest news.

"So, you mean to tell me," the heavyset Munson said, smoking away at his stogie. "The last-minute Anglophone event has been cancelled?"

"Anglophone is ill."

"I've seen him around town and he's as healthy as a horse. Word is, he is having it off with a young girl he brought back from the city. She's living at his place. God knows what Anglophone is up to," Munson said, then puffed out a smoke ring and watched it billow.

"Well, we'll have to wait to find out. And when they reschedule, I'll be sure to get in there and get you a scoop. I might check the girl out. I wonder if she knows about Anglophone's history?"

"No one could pin the murder on him for the last one, but he was under suspicion. If it weren't for his money, paying everyone off, they would have charged him. After all, the woman was murdered on his premises. The two of them were the only ones with keys to the library. He also looked guilty as hell. I, for one, would sure like to blow this case wide open and get the woman some justice."

"My dad felt Anglophone was definitely hiding something. The truth will probably never be known," Viveca said with remorse. "This new girl up there with him, I don't like it."

"That poor girl!" Munson said, unable to hide his excitement at this new information any longer. "Let's get in there and see what we can find out. Hey, why don't you start taking a walk up that way, see if you can spot her. Suss out the situation. Can you do that, Hartman?"

"I'll do what I can. I want to keep it low key," Viveca said with conviction.

"If anyone can find out what's going on, it's you," Munson said as he stubbed the lit part of the cigar.

"Is your wife still rationing them?" Viveca inquired with a smirk.

"Yes, but what she doesn't know won't hurt her."

"Righto." Viveca headed for the exit.

Munson put the partially smoked cigar back in its cellophane wrapping. "Oh, and report to me on this once a day—let's try to nail this s.o.b."

"Yes, Sir," Viveca closed the door behind her.

She felt incredibly happy about her conversation with Munson because he had a lot of faith in her ability. She had come up without much experience, but with connections and a strong desire to be a reporter. She had worked her way up from proofreading to the social page, but she wanted more.

This is my shot and I'm not going to blow it!

Viveca, who lived alone in a two-story apartment building in Port Dover, got into her car and drove home. She made her way up the stairs, thinking about how glad she was to live alone. She planned on a quiet evening in.

It was unexpected for her, to come home and find her dad waiting. Her father lived in Brantford, forty-five minutes away.

"Hi Dad," Viveca said.

"Viv, good to see you. I was hoping we could have dinner tonight," Frank Hartman said. From behind his back, he revealed a large bouquet of flowers. "I thought these might cheer up your table."

"Beans on toast tonight, Dad," Viveca said. He stood and she kissed him on the top of his bald head.

"Oh, that's a gourmet meal then." Frank laughed too and moved aside so his daughter could get by to unlock the front door. "You know, Viv, if you got your dear old Dad a copy of your key, then I could cook us a gourmet something, and surprise you. Scrambled eggs on toast."

They laughed, happy to be in each other's company.

"But, Dad," Viveca teased, "what if I was on a date? You'd feel terrible for intruding and I'd feel so guilty."

"Ah, if you had a date, I'd be happy to see you go out. I'm proud of you, Viv, but I do think you're being wasted on that society page. You deserve more."

"I know, I know, Dad," Viveca said, as she plopped the baked beans into a microwave dish and set the timer for two minutes. She popped two slices of bread into the toaster and pushed the lever down. "Two minutes to dinner. Cabernet Sauvignon, okay? Or do you prefer Chardonnay?" When the two minutes were up, she gave the beans a stir, then popped them back into the microwave for another thirty seconds.

"A bottle of beer would suit me fine." Frank popped a can of beer open for himself. "Cold beer and baked beans on toast with HP Sauce on the side—you can't get much more gourmet than that!"

Viveca buttered the toast, then poured the baked beans over the slices. It was a British dish, her mother's favourite. She and her father often shared it. Without mentioning her name, it was like her mother was sitting at the table with them.

Frank retrieved cutlery from the drawer, and they sat down to eat.

"So, what's new with you?" he asked.

"Nothing much, other than work. I'm on a new story. How about you, Dad? What's new with you?"

"My life is same, same, but that new story sounds interesting. Tell me more."

"I hate to talk business with you Dad. Surely you must have something interesting to tell me. What's happening in your garden? Is Old Lady Warner still chasing you around the neighbourhood?"

Frank put his knife and fork on the side of his plate. Downed a few gulps of beer.

"Sorry, now I've embarrassed you." Viveca poured some more wine into her glass and took a sip. "Alright, we'll talk about me. About work. My story is about Theodore Anglophone."

"What's he up to this time?"

"Funny you should say that. Do you still see him very often, Dad?"

"Not recently. He's been pretty much of a recluse since the incident at the library. He goes into the city where he's not so well known. I've heard he has another young girl staying with him, Viv. Is that true?" He took another slug of beer, his eyes fixed on Viv's face.

"It's true, and my boss has asked me to find out about her."

Frank gulped, almost choking. "Well, you don't want Anglophone as an enemy, not in this town, Viv. So, tread lightly. Remember you can catch more flies with honey than with vinegar. An old saying, but absolutely true." He coughed to clear his thoughts and then took another mouthful of food.

"I know, Daddy. I don't want to risk this opportunity either. Like you said, I need to get off the social page and onto something else, something more challenging. Something more ME." She moved the food around her plate, her thoughts lost on the prospect of a new story that could change her life.

"I'll help in any way I can. But I've always thought that woman dying in the library was negligence on Anglophone's part. There had to have been a cover up. It doesn't make sense, why someone would rob a library and tie her up. Maybe we did that woman wrong by letting him say what he did about her. I never felt right about it even though Anglophone and I have been acquaintances for years. He hasn't been himself since then—running to get women, bringing them back. Taking them out, parading them around like show horses. It's downright shameful," he said, sniffing as though a bad smell had invaded his nostrils.

"I know, Dad. Thanks for the advice. Now I'm tired and want to get to bed. Are you spending the night?"

"After two beers, I sure wouldn't want to drive."

"Guest room it is then. Leave the dishes."

"You ought to get a dishwasher."

"I already have one! Night, Dad," Viveca said, as she kissed her father on the cheek.

"Night, Love."

Chapter Fifty-One

ON THE WAY BACK to her room after breakfast the phone rang in the corridor and Ribby picked it up.

"Stephen?" Pause from a woman's voice. "Stephen?"

Ribby opened her mouth, but before she could say anything Tibbles snatched the phone out of her hand.

"Hello?" Tibbles waited. "This is the Anglophone residence." Someone was there. He could hear them breathing. "Miss Angela, you are not to answer the phone in this house. You are a, a, resident, and we are the staff. Please allow us to do our jobs."

"Excuse me, Tibbles."

Tibbles cradled the phone in his hand. "Did the person on the other end say anything?"

"Not a thing," Ribby said as she walked away.

"If you'd like some company Miss, Abbey is at your disposal."

"No thank you. I wish to walk on my own."

Once she was gone, Tibbles put the phone up to his ear again. Shallow breathing. "Rosemary?"

"Yes."

"I told you not to call here."

"I know, but I'm desperate. I have to get out of this godforsaken place. I'm going mad."

Tibbles paced, speaking as quietly as he could. "You simply must ask him to help you."

"I did, and he offered to send me some books. I don't need books to distract me I need to get out of here. I could go abroad. No one would know me."

"I can't help you. I have to go." He motioned to put down the phone.

"Wait!" Rosemary exclaimed.

He moved the phone back to his ear again. "You know, what he did to me."

Tibbles hesitated. "I have to go. Don't ring here again." He hung up.

Tibbles went to the front window and looked out. Ribby was sitting in a chair on the front porch. He went into the kitchen.

Do you think we should tell Stephen about the phone call?

I'm not sure.

Perhaps the caller doesn't like Tibbles either.

Hm, you could be right about that.

Ribby pointed herself in the direction of the limousine. As she drew near, she was able to see Stephen asleep behind the wheel with his chauffeur's cap over his eyes.

Ribby leaned in through the open window.

If we must awaken him, at least do it with a kiss. No one would know.

She cleared her throat. Have you lost your mind?

Check out those lips though. "Wakey wakey," Angela said as Stephen stirred and removed the hat from his face.

Stephen did a double take.

"A few moments ago, a woman asked for you on the phone."

"Oh?"

"Tibbles grabbed it out of my hand. She must've hung up then."

Stephen gripped the steering wheel.

"All she said was your name."

"Did you tell him that she asked for me?"

"No."

"Thank you for telling me." His arm brushed Ribby's elbow. "Oh, sorry."

"Uh, that's fine." She paused and leaned in, curiosity getting the better of her, "So, you know who it was?"

"Yes, Miss. It was my mom."

Chapter Fifty-Two

TIBBLES' STERN AND RIGID version of a Spidey-sense was tingling. He was certain Angela had lied, but why? He moved to a window in the front room as Angela was walking away. He continued to watch her. She stopped to chat with Stephen. Interesting. When had they become friends? Or had they?

Then he realised what was going on. When Miss Angela answered the phone, Rosemary had spoken. In fact, she'd spoken Stephen's name and now Miss Angela was out there conveying this message. Even more interesting.

Tibbles thought the best thing to do was to keep the lad occupied. He decided to assign Stephen a task.

Anglophone had been very clear. He was not to be disturbed. He'd fill him in, in due time. Praise or even a monetary reward might even be in order.

Tibbles continued through the house, finding Abbey hard at work dusting. He entreated her to go out and keep Miss Angela company during her walk.

"If she went out alone Mr. Tibbles, Miss Angela probably wants to be on her own."

"Did she order you not to join her?" Tibbles urged her to put down her dusting cloth and remove her apron.

"No, Sir," Abbey said. Her feet shuffled along as she made her way.

Tibbles shouted, "Pick up your feet you, silly girl."

He conducted her to and out the front door.

"Yes, Mr. Tibbles," Abbey said.

Unable to spot Angela, she asked Stephen where she was.

Stephen pointed. "I do think she wanted some alone time though."

"That's what I told Mr. Tibbles—he insisted."

Stephen laughed.

***

Stephen watched Abbey walk away thinking about Tibbles. No wonder the staff at the house had such a high turnover. Others weren't like him. Others didn't owe Anglophone everything. Without Anglophone he could never afford to keep his mother in such an expensive care centre.

His glance followed Abbey as she drew nearer to Angela who was now looking out over the water. As she neared the edge, a protective instinct in him made him worry she might fall.

His phone rang. A Tibbles summoning. He made his way inside.

"Stephen, I need you to pick up a few things," Tibbles said, standing over Stephen to enforce his authority. "Mr. Anglophone is indisposed. Here's the list."

Tibbles handed it over. Stephen glanced at the note before putting it into his jacket pocket.

"It will give you something to do, since you're unoccupied."

"No problem, Mr. Tibbles." Stephen exited. He'd get the things and then be straight back alright, after he checked on his mother.

Chapter Fifty-Three

THE NEXT DAY, VIVECA decided to venture into the Anglophone area. She'd take the scenic route along the waterfront. She cranked open her window and put her sunglasses on. The sun was high, the clouds were few. Wildflowers were scattered along the roadside, purples, yellows, and blues.

The drive was pleasant enough, with little traffic. As she turned the corner to the spot with the most spectacular view, she noticed a young woman she'd never seen before.

That must be her. She slowed down to a crawl.

A second girl met up with the first. Younger. The two embraced then walked along the pathway.

Viveca pulled over and parked her car under a very leafy maple. She walked some distance in her shoes with high heels, closing the gap between herself and the two women. When she was near enough for them to hear her, she shouted, "*Ouch!*" and went down.

They hadn't heard her. She tried again. "HELP!"

The two girls turned and made their way to her. She reached into her handbag and pressed record. *Okay kid, here they come, so you better make this good.* She rubbed her ankle with her one hand to raise the blood to the surface and brushed away crocodile tears with the other.

"Do you need an ambulance?" Ribby asked.

"Oh, I'm such a klutz," Viveca said. She attempted to stand up. "My ankle, I think it's sprained. I was having visions of being stuck out here all night with coyotes howling all around me until I spotted you two."

"What an imagination," Ribby said as she bent down to have a look.

Abbey did the same. It looked a bit red.

"My name is Viveca, Viveca Hartman, by the way." She extended her hand.

"I'm Abbey, and this is Angela. Pl-leased to meet you."

A seagull swooped around Viveca's head, annoying her with a squawk. She shooed it away.

"Oh, may I?" Abbey asked.

Viveca nodded.

Abbey bent down and massaged it for a few seconds. "There now, is that any better?"

"Yes, thanks," Viveca said.

"Where's your car?" Ribby asked.

"I parked it over there in the shade." Abbey helped Viveca as she attempted to stand. When she was up-right she said, "I'm a reporter, you see, and I'm doing a story on Natural Wonders. I've heard the view from up here is spectacular."

"It is," Ribby said. "Next time you should wear more appropriate shoes."

Yeah, like you did when you walked all the way back from the library.

Shut up.

They helped Viveca to her car.

"It was lovely to meet you and thank you so much for helping this damsel in distress. Oh, here's my business card in case you ever want to get in touch."

"Thank you. Are you sure you can drive, okay?" Abbey asked.

"Yes, thank you. Oh, since it's nearby, I wondered if you girls knew anything about the library. I heard it might be opening again?"

"No, we don't know anything about it," Ribby said.

"Well, it has been closed for years. Under suspicious circumstances. Makes you wonder about the new Librarian."

"What are you insinuating?" Ribby asked.

"Only wondering if she, I mean the new Librarian…"

"What makes you think the new Librarian is a woman?" Ribby asked.

"Oh, rumours. I'd sure like to talk to her. Maybe even do an interview for the paper."

"Sorry, we can't help you. We must get back now. Good luck with your article."

"I hope your ankle gets better soon," Abbey added.

"Ah, yes, thanks for your help. Hope to see you again sometime."

Once Viveca was in her car, Abbey and Ribby walked away.

"Very strange," Ribby said, glancing back over her shoulder.

"I wouldn't give it another thought," Abbey replied.

"I know," Ribby said with a furrowed brow. "I feel like she already knew who I was. Like she was on a fishing expedition."

"You're right, but she's gone now. Besides, I bet Tibbles is champing at the bit back there waiting for me. I don't think he expected me to be out of the house this long."

"Oh, he wanted you to trail me. You're his little spy," Ribby said as she put her arm around Abbey's shoulder.

"I'd never," she said, aghast at the suggestion.

"Of course, but he doesn't know we're friends."

"Well, I definitely won't be telling him about that reporter."

"I'll let Mr. Anglophone know we met her up here. It's none of Tibbles' business."

They rounded the pathway leading up to the front of the mansion and went inside.

Chapter Fifty-Four

STEPHEN ARRIVED AT THE hospital and asked to see his mother. His request was denied. He became agitated and caused a scene.

Two big burly bouncer-type staffers lifted him off the ground from behind and removed him from the premises.

"Ring my employer, Mr. Theodore Anglophone. Ring him!"

"Sure, we'll do that," the smaller of the two men said as Stephen's body landed with a thump on the tarmac.

His tires squealed as he pulled away from the hospital. He'd floor it all the way back to the estate. He didn't care how many stones bounced off the car along the way.

***

VIVECA THUMPED HER HANDS on the steering wheel. Her plan had not gone well. She hoped she hadn't blown the entire deal.

I need to warn that girl, so I'll have to talk to Dad and see if he can help me to get my foot in the door, Viveca thought. *If I keep on like this, I'm never going to get promoted.*

She set her phone so any calls would automatically go to speaker phone. She moved her seat closer as she pulled out of the parking spot under the tree. Nearly all the way back now, her phone rang and opened the line.

An on-coming black-stretch limousine crossed over the centreline and into her lane.

The limo driver's eyes bulged, and he cranked his wheel at the same time as she did. The two cars passed within an inch of each other.

"Whoa! Watch it! You, crazy bastard!" Viveca shouted.

"I sure hope you're not talking to me," Munson said.

"Uh no, boss, it was Anglophone's chauffeur. He nearly took me out!"

"What's up with him?"

"No idea, but I'm sure glad we're going in opposite directions."

"So, did you find her?"

"I did."

"And?"

"I made a bit of a production out of it. Pretended to sprain my ankle."

"Oh boy. Did she buy it?"

"It seemed to be convincing enough."

"And what was she like?"

"Her name is Angela. Seemed nice, albeit naive."

"Not a social climber then? Or a local?"

"No, not at all. She's different. I figure she's around thirty something, quiet, soft spoken. Hope I didn't push too hard and turn her off."

"Damn it, Viveca, your social page training should teach you how to handle sticky situations. I hope you didn't blow it and if you did, FIX IT."

"Sure thing, boss," she said as he disconnected. She headed home.

***

Back at the house, Stephen decided to go straight inside and confess to Anglophone. If he faced the music, admitted his indiscretion then Anglophone would be understanding. Anglophone had a soft spot for his mother. He'd help to sort it out.

Then again, if he mentioned the phone call, he'd give Miss Angela away; that she'd come to him and told him about the call.

So, I can't mention the call. I'll have to tell him I had a gut feeling Mom was in danger. A son's instinct. I had to go and see her then and there. Surely Anglophone will be able to forgive me.

Stephen went inside. There was no one around. He returned his post.

Chapter Fifty-Five

Anglophone awoke and bellowed for Tibbles.

Tibbles was in the kitchen, cross-examining Abbey. Anglophone's continuous bell ringing diverted his attention.

Tibbles pointed his finger into Abbey's face. "We're not finished! Don't move! That's an order!"

When he arrived at Anglophone's door, something hard crashed inside. Tibbles pushed the door open and what a sight he did see.

A more than usually impatient Anglophone had pulled the bell ringer apparatus from the ceiling. There he sat, red-faced amongst the plaster and rubble.

"I'm sorry, Sir,' Tibbles said.

Anglophone glared and shouted. "Of course, you are Tibbles. You're always sorry, but that's beside the point. Now tell me why the hospital called me on my private number to complain about one of my employees?" He paused for effect and when there was no reaction from Tibbles.

"I, I..."

"Stephen caused quite a ruckus."

"I, I..."

"You Tibbles, what do you have to say for yourself? Why are you sending my staff gallivanting about on *my time?* Or did my chauffeur drive off my premises of his own volition? Explain yourself, man!"

"I, we needed some things for the household. You were indisposed. Stephen was unoccupied. He had specific instructions. I had no idea he would abuse my trust." He paused. Perspiration dripped down his forehead. "Your trust. He is an impertinent...."

"That he is, but you, Tibbles, are a bumbling fool! Now you reprimand Stephen. Put him to work cutting grass for the next fortnight and get me another driver to replace him. And a pay cut. He will get fifty dollars less pay, and as his accomplice, so will you. Get someone up here and fix this thing...and don't forget the sleeping pills. Now go before I make it one hundred!"

***

Sometime later, Ribby was sound asleep on the floor of the library in the house with open books framing her form.

The sleeping pills which Anglophone had asked Tibbles to place in her tea had been effective. All he needed was a few minutes to get a sample while they were fixing up his room and then he'd know if Angela was his daughter.

Anglophone stood over her, looking at her, wanting her so badly that he ached. He couldn't be this girl's father. It was impossible. The mere idea he could be attracted to his own flesh and blood...

As he gazed upon her, a memory of Martha returned. She had told the truth. They had met before. Why, until she mentioned it, had he not remembered her? Memories were like that as you aged, they came and went without rhyme or reason.

He caressed Ribby's hair, wondering. He continued touching the back of her hand, as he rolled up the sleeve of her blouse.

The vial was waiting, and the needle was ready.

Wake up, Ribby. Wake up! The old bastard is. He's....

"My dear, Angela," Anglophone whispered as he jabbed the point of the needle into her vein. The blood flowed into the vial. He looked at her wound and bent over her, licking the open sore with his tongue. The blood tasted sweet, like Angela. He could feel the stiffening in his pants and knew he had to get out of there. He hated to see her so uncomfortable on the floor all night.

He gathered up the sample and put labels onto the bottle. He picked up her phone which was sitting on the table.

Tibbles stood outside the door as Anglophone exited. "The vehicle you ordered is awaiting instruction."

"One moment," Anglophone secured the samples into the cooler bag. He handed them to Tibbles. "Tell the driver to go straight to the lab. I've already informed my contact at the lab that this is high priority. I expect an immediate answer." He paused. "When you're finished, take her up to her room. Oh and," he handed Tibbles her phone. "Put this away somewhere safe until I tell you otherwise."

Tibbles nodded, "I've been hiding it, every now and then, as you asked me to, but this will make it more permanent." Then he made his way to the front of the house.

Anglophone returned to his room. He was hungry, but the late Afternoon Tea in the garden would sort it out. In the meantime, he would not get a moment of peace until he knew for sure if he was in love with his own daughter.

Chapter Fifty-Six

Tired of waiting for the axe to fall, Stephen slammed the car door and after grabbing the bag of things he'd purchased for Tibbles he stormed inside. He stopped mid-stride when he encountered Tibbles.

Tibbles bellowed, "There you are, you imbecile! Get in my office, NOW!"

"Not now, you blowhard, get out of my way. I need to see Anglophone."

Tibbles raised his hand to slap Stephen's face.

Stephen blocked the blow and the two men locked eyes. Stephen held onto Tibbles' hand for a few seconds then let it drop.

The two men stood eye to eye, noses nearly touching in a battle of who would give in first.

"Sorry, Tibbles," Stephen said.

"I should say so. Apology accepted. Now, go into my office and wait for me. I have business to attend to first, then we can sort this out."

Tibbles left the house. He leaned into the open window of the waiting car, conveying Anglophone's instructions. The car sped away. Tibbles returned to his office.

"Sit down, Stephen, please." Tibbles paced for a few seconds before he spoke. "Mr. Anglophone is extremely agitated. Number one; he is cross at me, because I let you gallivant around on his time. Number two; he is cross at you, because the hospital complained about the scene you caused. What the blazes were you thinking?"

"I had a feeling Mother was unwell. I had to check it out. To see if she was okay."

"Lies, all lies," Tibbles said under his breath. "I know Miss Angela told you about the phone call. Dare you deny it?"

Stephen looked at his feet.

"Your demeanor tells all! So, when I asked you to go and get some things, you intended to abuse my trust."

"I'm sorry Tibbles. I am, but I had to go."

"Well, Mr. Anglophone has suspended you for two weeks. Because I put my trust in you, he has deducted my pay also. Moreover, you will be a dog's body around here—cutting the lawn, doing whatever tasks are allotted to you. I need to hire another driver. With any luck the new man will not be as impertinent as you!"

"I'm sorry your pay was docked. I don't think that's fair. I can talk to him about it."

"You will not."

"Withhold my pay, but please don't leave me without a vehicle. Let me go and talk to him. I'll beg his forgiveness."

"Mr. Anglophone says he doesn't wish to speak with you for a fortnight. If you see him, keep working. Show your dedication. Show him remorse. We're lucky he didn't fire us. In time things will return to their normal state."

Tibbles picked up the phone and ignored Stephen's presence.

Stephen, uncertain what to do now, put his head into his hands. Tibbles chatted away on the phone. Dejected, he got up and left the office. He ventured outside with his fists clenched deep in his pockets.

He meandered for hours, taking in the views, and weighing things up in his mind.

He had to figure out how to get his mother out of that place.

He had to find a way to be independent from Anglophone.

He had to take control of his life. If he could only figure out how.

Chapter Fifty-Seven

RIBBY OPENED HER EYES. At first, she didn't know where she was. The last thing she remembered was reading in the library.

She attempted to sit up, but her head hurt, and the room spun. She hugged herself and noticed a big purple splotchy bruise on her arm. She tried to remember an occasion in which the bruise might have occurred. She failed.

Angela couldn't remember anything either. There was something bugging her. A faint memory, unattainable.

How could this have happened?

You probably walked into something. It wouldn't be the first time.

True enough, I can be a klutz.

Don't worry about it. You have more important fish to fry.

Ribby smelled the alluded to fish frying and ran down the hall into the bathroom to be sick. She washed her face and drank a few sips of water.

Better now?

I think so, thanks.

Where is Teddy anyway? It's almost like he's losing interest. You had him in the palm of your hand.

He's a busy man.

Ribby cleaned herself up and brushed her teeth.

Besides, he hasn't been well.

Something still nagged Angela. Something she was near to remembering, but then it slipped away.

But he's a man and you must keep him interested. Flirt a little. Add a little sex appeal. Keep him guessing and hoping. Mind you, I'm not suggesting you go all the way anytime soon. Play him.

I don't have much experience in the man department.

I think he's a horny old codger at heart.

He wants someone to be there for him. Someone he can count on.

He could have his pick with all that money. So, don't blow it kid— or if you do, make it count!!

You are so disgusting.

"Miss Angela, Miss Angela," Abbey called as she rapped on the door.

"Mr. Anglophone is waiting for you in the garden."

"Come on in, Abbey. I'm not feeling up to Afternoon Tea."

"You must."

Ribby sat down on the bed holding her head in her hands.

"Please tell Mr. Anglophone to meet me in one hour's time."

"As you will, Miss Angela."

"Once you're finished, come back and help me get ready."

"Sure thing, Miss Angela. I'll be right back."

A few moments later, Abbey returned to Ribby's room.

"I hope Mr. Anglophone wasn't cross with me," Ribby said.

"No, Miss Angela. He understands we take longer to make ourselves presentable," she said with a laugh. "Now sit yourself down here and let me help you." Abbey chattered away, while Ribby allowed herself to be pampered. "Voila," she said.

"Thank you, Abbey."

"You look wonderful!" Abbey said as they made their way along the corridor and outside into the garden.

Ribby spotted Teddy with his face obscured behind a newspaper. She quietly sat down next to him. He had not heard her. She smiled.

Tibbles stormed to the table and announced, "Good afternoon, Miss Angela."

Teddy nearly dropped the newspaper when he stood up. "How long have you been sitting there?"

"Actually, it was only a few moments. Did you miss me?" Ribby whispered, taking his hand into hers.

Anglophone pulled his hand away and said, "I was very, very ill."

Ribby's complexion burned.

What the?

"But I did think of you, often."

"And what did you think about me?"

"I thought about you and the library."

"Exactly, and I have some ideas I want to discuss with you."

"Where did Tibbles get to? TIBBLES!"

Tibbles returned. Abbey trailed behind. They carried trays filled with food and beverages. Anglophone's plate was soon filled with food, while Ribby chose a strong cup of tea.

"I've been thinking," Ribby said, stirring her tea. "I'd like to read to and perform for children in the library. I'd like to make plans for a Children's Day."

"And what would that entail?"

"Authors could do book-readings."

"Hmmm, interesting, interesting," Teddy said.

"Also, I'd like us to donate books to hospitals."

"Yes, I like those ideas, my Angel, it will take some thought, some organizing. For now, we ought to concentrate on the library. Once we're up and running, perhaps in a year or two, then you can implement those other ideas. Go slowly, Angela. Remember this isn't a big city. We're talking a different breed of people here."

"Families are everywhere."

"I see your point," Teddy said, patting Ribby's hand like a child he needed to supplicate.

"Excuse me," a man with cap in hand said from the entranceway.

"Yes? Oh, I see, you're the new chauffeur."

Tibbles entered clicking his heels. "I told you to wait for me in the kitchen."

My apologies," the new man said as he tipped his cap first to Anglophone and then to Tibbles. He backed himself out of the room.

"Is Stephen ill?"

"No. He isn't." Teddy took a bite of quiche. "He abused my trust. He's in the doghouse for the next fortnight."

"I'm sorry to hear that." She took a sip of tea. "I'd like to call my mother, and I seem to have misplaced my cellphone."

"Certainly. Use the phone in the entryway. Meanwhile, we'll check around and see if we can find your phone."

Ribby was so happy that she stood up, dropping her napkin onto the ground, and rushed over to Teddy. She flew at him, filled with passion, put her arms around his neck, and kissed him on the lips. She opened her eyes. He was looking back at her. He was stone cold.

He pushed her away and stood. His face was red.

Ribby ran out of the room and up the stairs. She threw herself onto her bed and cried herself to sleep.

You call that sexy?

Chapter Fifty-Eight

THE NEXT MORNING, after she opened the balcony doors, Ribby stretched and yawned. The sunlight warmed her skin, and she felt a strong yearning to be closer to the waterfront. She dressed, showered, then threw on her hat, pinched her cheeks, and made her way out of the mansion.

On the pathway, she spotted Stephen. He had his back to her, but she could hear the clipping sounds of the shears. He was trimming the rose bushes.

"Stephen," Ribby said.

He straightened his back and held his hand in the air to shade the sunrays from his eyes.

"I wondered if you could drive me somewhere."

He did not answer. Instead, he turned back around and resumed his gardening chores. He waited for her to walk away, kept snipping and clipping. After a moment or two he said, "Why me? Ask the old man. I can't help you. I can't even help myself."

"But I have no one, Stephen." She touched his shoulder. "I want to go home."

He turned toward her abruptly, nearly causing her to lose her balance. "I can't help you. Damn it. I would like to, honestly, I would, but I...There are other people depending on me. I cannot help you. Now GO AWAY!"

Ribby stepped back, fighting the urge to cry. "I only thought...I'm sorry for troubling you."

Stephen let her go. He let her get further and further away before he called out. Ribby ignored him. He ran after her.

"Look, I'm sorry. His eyes met hers. "It's just that I've been demoted, and I really hate gardening."

Ribby took in his softened features.

He glanced back at the house nervously as a car sped by them. The driver got out and ran up the stairs where Tibbles opened the door. A few moments later the car sped by them on the way out.

Ribby moved in on Stephen.

Stephen moved in on Ribby.

They met somewhere in the middle.

Chapter Fifty-Nine

TIBBLES DELIVERED THE ENVELOPE to Anglophone then returned to his duties.

Anglophone was at the window, watching his now confirmed daughter and son as they made googly eyes at each other. He could feel the chemistry between them all the way in his room. He laughed as he watched them whisper and exchange glances.

He rang the bell and Tibbles returned within seconds.

"Tibbles," Teddy said, "I'm going to the city today. I have a few things to attend to there. Alert the driver—I will return tomorrow.

"In the meantime, watch Stephen and Miss Angela for me. See what they get up to, but don't let them know you're watching." He touched his nose with his index finger. "Discretion, my dear Tibbles, discretion."

"Of course, Mr. Anglophone." Tibbles bowed his way out of the room.

Chapter Sixty

"How can I help you?" Stephen said, leading Ribby away from the main pathway. "Like I said, I can't even help myself. I have responsibilities."

Tibbles honed-in on them as Anglophone readied to depart.

"Is it something to do with your mother?"

"I can't tell you. The less you know the better. Why do you want to leave? Has he done something to you?"

"I don't even know what I'm doing here," Ribby said. "I mean, why me?"

The limousine sped away.

"Wonder where he's off to."

"He has a new driver."

"I know but it's only temporary," Stephen said. "If you need to get away, do it now."

"How can I? I don't have a car."

Ribby, you are totally panicking. Calm down.

"Surely, you must know someone up here, who could help."

"I met a reporter yesterday, Viveca Something."

"Yes, call her. Ask her."

"What if she won't come?"

"Trust me, she will," Stephen said.

"How do you know? Why would she care about me?"

"Didn't she ask you a bunch of questions about Anglophone?"

"Not really," Ribby said. "She said she was writing a story about natural wonders."

"You may think that, but trust me, you're the story. Besides the reporters, you can guarantee the police are keeping an eye on the situation, too."

"I don't get it. Why?"

"All I can tell you Miss, is to call her. Let the reporter explain. But don't say anything about me, I'm in enough trouble already. And for God's sake, don't ring from the house. You need a cellphone, or better still, can you trust Abbey? I mean, *really* trust Abbey?"

"I had a cell, but I lost it. Regarding Abbey, yes, I think so," Ribby said. "I'm pretty sure I could trust her with my life."

"Then use her. Get her to go and ring the reporter. I'd let you do mine, but Tibbles probably has it tapped. Do it today, Miss."

"Thank you," Ribby said as she touched his hand.

"Okay, I'll see you around then," Stephen said. He glanced up at the window, noticed the curtains moving. Tibbles. He returned to pruning the roses.

Such a cute butt.

Don't you ever think of anything else?

Stephen turned around, looked at Ribby and then went back to work again.

Ribby searched for Abbey.

When they nearly collided in the main corridor, Abbey said, "Tibbles said I had to find you, IMMEDIATELY. I don't know what the fuss is all about. Just because Mr. Anglophone is away for a day or two."

"Yes, I saw his car just now."

"I'm to be your shadow."

Ribby and Abbey went out the door and kept on going. When they were far enough away from the mansion Ribby said, "I want to get away from here and I need your help."

"If Tibbles finds out he'll be very cross. He might even fire me."

"I need you to call someone. That woman we met yesterday, you know, the reporter?" Abbey nodded. "I need you to go to a phone, not here, anywhere else but here, and for you to ring her. Make an appointment for us to meet. Will you do it?"

"I can do that," Abbey said after some hesitation. "In fact, I'm going to Fairfield Farm down the road to get some cheese. The driver was meant to take me, but now I need to walk. I can ring her from there."

"You're a star," Ribby said. "Now, I'll get back inside. Have fun at Fairfield Farm."

"When should I set it up? I mean the meeting with you and Viveca?"

"I think she will know how difficult it may be for me. Tell her though that Mr. Anglophone is away, and ASAP would be best."

"It's a plan."

***

At Fairfield Farm Abbey dialed Viveca Hartman's number at the newspaper. "Uh, hello, it's me, Abbey."

"Abbey who?" Viveca said crossly. "You have Viveca Hartman at The Local Times here."

"Yes, I know, uh, h-how's your ankle?"

"My ankle? I..." Viveca caught on. "Abbey, oh yes. What can I do for you? Is it Angela? Is she alright?"

"Yes," Abbey said, "and I've been worried sick about you, being so ill and then spraining your ankle like that."

"Okay," Viveca said, "someone else is there, is that right?"

"Oh, my yes," Abbey said, "you really have to take it easy and keep off of it."

"Abbey," Viveca said, "I, don't know what you want or how I can help. Uh, does she want to see me? Does Angela want me to come out there?"

"Yes," Abbey said, "Mr. Anglophone is away in the city. As soon as possible would be best. I'm at Fairfield Farm now, picking up some cheese."

"Okay, Abbey," Viveca said, "What about tomorrow, between 10 and 11 a.m.?"

"We'll try to get away. Please wait for us at Fairfield Farm, even if we're late."

"Will do," Viveca replied.

Chapter Sixty-One

At 9 p.m. Anglophone's limousine rounded the corner on the way to Martha's house. It was his favourite time of year when it was still light in the evening. True, she was in prison, but he wanted to see if he could find out anything from the neighbours. He was still infuriated Martha had snuck back into his life. He'd opened his library and his heart and now...

Martha's house was gone. Totally obliterated. All that remained was a pile of scorched rubble. He stepped out of the car to take a closer look. The chauffeur stood at his side.

An elderly woman meandered along the pavement. She was wearing a tatty bathroom robe. She approached Anglophone. The driver put his body between himself and the woman.

"Damn shame," the woman said, trying to move closer to Anglophone. "Such a good woman and to go like that. So sad. And her poor daughter. No one knows where she is and now, now all the scandal. I don't know. I just don't know." She dabbed her eyes with the corner of her sleeve as she glanced toward the limousine.

"Are you suggesting that the woman who lived here, Martha, died?"

"No, she didn't die. Her neighbour Mrs. Engle smelled smoke. She pulled Martha and Scamp's bodies out of there. Saved their lives even though Martha didn't want to live. Scamp's been adopted by Mrs. Engle." She pointed to the house.

"What do you mean, she didn't want to live?"

"She was full of pills and booze."

"Please continue."

"The house went up like a tinderbox. We were never friends. That woman had men coming and going all the time. It was like her house had a revolving door." The woman scratched herself, like she had fleas. "I'd best get inside before I catch my death. Evening, Sir." She walked away.

"Wait. Stay. Come inside my car and I'll give you a nip of whiskey to warm you up," Anglophone said.

The woman stopped. She turned toward him. She hesitated, then walked away.

"I'd really appreciate your help," Anglophone called. "I'll make it worth your while."

"Uh, but I, I don't know you from Adam," the woman said. "You could be one of Martha's degenerate friends. Wanting a piece of this." She waved her arms and smiled, revealing a toothless grin.

"Well, I'm Theodore Anglophone, an old friend of Martha's. We go a long way back." He slipped a twenty into her palm.

"She's in jail."

He waved a fifty in front of her face, which she tried to grab.

"Steady on, friend," Anglophone said. "Tell me something worth fifty dollars. I work hard for my money."

"I can tell you things; things which would make your head spin."

Anglophone moved closer and the pungent smell of cabbage made him cover his nose with his hand. "Your carriage awaits."

The elderly woman laughed as the chauffeur opened the door for her.

Once they were inside, Teddy filled a glass with whiskey and then handed it to the woman. She knocked it back. He refilled it.

"Well, Martha and Ribby lived here, and Martha was a prostitute, although from what I heard not a very well paid one." She laughed. "We knew about it; all her neighbours knew, that is. We turned a blind eye to it. So long as she stayed away from our husbands, it was live and let live. Then the papers found out and came here to check out the whorehouse. Ribby wasn't around then, bless her soul. Poor little mite though. What she must've seen with men coming and going when she was growing up."

"Yes, get to the point, to earn the fifty dollars," Anglophone demanded.

"When the house burned to the ground, they found…Something…In the shed…Later…While Martha was recovering in the hospital…"

"Get to it."

The woman held out her glass. When it was full, she continued. "That's when they found it, a knife."

"Oh, my," Teddy said, leaning closer to the woman. He refilled her glass.

"So, there she was, poor Martha, without her daughter, without a soul, and they charged her with first degree. Two murders. Her sister and one of her Johns—I think he was Thursday's. It was all over the newspapers. It was crazy around here."

"Thursday's?" Teddy said in a revolted tone.

The woman hesitated, "Fat, very, very, fat. Not your ordinary kind of fat. Very unattractive. And married too."

"Get on with the story. Then what happened?" Teddy asked impatiently.

"He was dead. Stabbed in the back. The papers reckoned the sisters had a fight over him." The woman cackled like a chicken laying an egg at the wonderment of women fighting over such a prize.

"She's in the penitentiary waiting for the judge to sentence her. They reckon she killed the man and her sister. Then she drove them off a cliff. They found the knife and one of her dresses covered in Carl Wheeler's blood buried in the shed out back." She stopped and waited in hope her tale had been enough to earn the fifty.

"You've been really helpful. Here's another one hundred for your time, and you can take the rest of the bottle with you, too."

When the woman didn't seem interested in getting out, the chauffeur opened the door. Anglophone gave her a little shove.

"Now, you didn't have to push! You, you!" the woman exclaimed, as she backed away from the car.

"Go on," Mr. Anglophone said to the driver when he returned to his seat. "Take me to the Penitentiary."

"Yes, Mr. Anglophone."

Teddy leaned back and closed his eyes.

Chapter Sixty-Two

THE FOLLOWING MORNING, RIBBY and Abbey met Viveca at Fairfield Farm.

"You look sensational!" Abbey said.

"Thanks, Ang," Viveca said. "I'm well enough to even hop up on one of those horses today and go for a ride. Provided you choose a gentle soul, riding would suit me fine."

"Abbey knows all our horses," Mrs. Fairfield said. "I hate to rush out, but I have a few chores to do in town. So, make yourselves at home. Help yourselves to anything you need. I should be back by lunchtime, if you'd like to stay?"

"No, thank you," the trio said in unison.

"Busy, busy, busy," Ribby said, and Abbey and Viveca nodded their heads in agreement.

After Mrs. Fairfield left the house, Viveca asked, "What's up?"

Abbey said, "I'll go out for a ride while you two talk."

"Thanks, Abbey. You're a gem," Ribby said as she watched Abbey close the door behind her. Ribby then focused her attention on Viveca, who seemed as anxious as she was.

"How can I help?" Viveca asked.

"First, thank you for coming at such short notice. I'm in over my head at the house with Mr. Anglophone. I want to go home."

"And he won't let you? You're being held prisoner?"

"Not exactly. He's been kind to me, up until a few days ago—even though I feel very isolated since he's always away on business. A couple of days ago, oh, I don't know how to explain it other than I wanted to leave. On top of that, my phone disappeared. I know he wants me to stay and open-up the Library, but I suspect he's hiding something from me. I don't know why he needs me to be the Librarian. I mean, me specifically. It's not like I answered an advertisement for the position. Quite frankly, I'm frightened."

"First, tell me what you know."

"I think you better just start from the very beginning."

"Anglophone has a reputation for the ladies. To put it simply, he fancies himself. With all that money, not to mention the power he wields, he's able to do things a normal man couldn't do. For example, he has several members of the Council in his back pocket. It's a known fact, he greases palms, but he's so powerful no one can get any evidence on him. Like what happened at the Library. I mean, Stephen's Mom was tied up and left for dead."

"That woman, was Stephen's Mom?"

But Stephen's Mom isn't dead...

"You mean you know about that, what happened before at the library?"

"Yes, I read about it online before I came here."

"But in the papers, they didn't tell the whole story. Like when the reporters arrived first and found her, she was in quite a state. Reporters talk and well, they say she was naked, tied to a chair with burns on her body and there was lots of blood. Forensics later discovered it was animal blood. Some say Anglophone was into black magic. Weird stuff."

Ribby remembered the silhouetted man on the back of the book about magic.

This doesn't make sense. Stephen visits her.

And she phoned him.

Viveca continued, "Yes, but there's more. Some say she was Anglophone's lover. She was definitely the only person he ever entrusted his library to."

This is getting more and more strange.

"My father goes a long way back with Anglophone, and Stephen has lived there since he was a boy."

"So, with me then, why me?"

"I don't know, but I don't blame you for wanting to go home. Don't you have any family?"

"Yes," Ribby said, "my mom is in the city. I need to call her. I'll call her from here right now." Ribby picked up the phone.

"I'm sorry, the number you are calling is no longer in service. Please hang up and dial again."

Ribby dialed again, with the same result.

"Maybe I can contact her for you? Get her to come to get you with reinforcements, i.e., cops. What's her name?"

"Martha, Martha Balustrade."

"Oh my God!" Viveca exclaimed. "You're not Martha Balustrade's Daughter!"

Oh, oh, what has Mommy Dearest done now?

Chapter Sixty-Three

TEDDY ARRIVED AT THE Penitentiary. Martha was being held in solitary confinement. He demanded to see her. He pretended to be her lawyer.

A woman at the desk was shuffling through papers. Anglophone banged his fist on her desk, reiterating his demands. "Call Frederick Schmidt. Call Mayor Brown. They know me. They will allow me to see my client, IMMEDIATELY," Anglophone bellowed.

Phone calls were made. Still Anglophone waited for hours.

"Can I get you a cup of tea?"

"No, thank you," Anglophone said, "seeing my client is all I want to do."

Chapter Sixty-Four

"YOU KNOW MY MOM?"

"He has been keeping you secluded," Viveca said. "E*veryone* knows about your mom, what with all the press lately. I mean, when someone confesses to the murders of two people including her own sister, it makes the news—even out here. Not to mention her other shenanigans. Front page in the city, Angela!" She watched as Ribby's face went white as a sheet. "I'm sorry, she is your mom, after-all."

"A murderer? You must be mistaken." She paused. "By the way, my real name is Ribby Balustrade."

"Then why?"

"It's an Anglophone thing."

"He made you change your name?"

"No, Angela is prettier than Ribby."

"Viveca isn't quite common or pretty either so I know what you mean. But let's get back to your mom and the murders. You don't think she did it?"

We know she didn't because we did it.

We did one; the other was suicide.

Ribby said nothing.

"Look, I know Anglophone has kept you secluded down here. You'd think he'd at least have the decency to tell you about your mother being in prison."

"I've been spending all of my time reading and fixing up the library. Meanwhile, my mother has been...Oh my God, I've got to go to her, now. Can you take me? You've got to help me. You've just got to!"

Abbey popped her head around the corner and heard Ribby's plea. "What's happening? Why is she so upset? Angela, what's wrong? You look like you've seen a ghost!"

"I need to go to the city, today. Now. Viveca is going to take me."

"My dad can probably get us onto a plane, and we'll be there in no time. Just a second, I'll give him a ring and explain. He's well versed in legal mumbo jumbo, so I'll see if he can join us."

"There's an airport nearby? Why doesn't Teddy fly to Toronto then? Surely he can afford it?"

"Afraid of flying," Viveca said, just as her dad picked up the phone at the other end. She explained everything to him. He agreed to meet them at the airport. "Okay ladies, off we go then!"

"Wait," Ribby said, "can we drop by and pickup Stephen too? I, I'd like him to be there."

"Sure, we'll swing by and if he wants to come, the more the merrier. What about you, Abbey? Are you joining us?"

"No, I can't afford to lose my job right now. Tibbles would simply hit the roof if I disappeared all day."

Abbey looked at her watch and started to get anxious. "I've been gone too long already."

"Hop in and I'll give you a lift."

"But, what about Tibbles?" Abbey asked. "If he asks me anything? I'm not a good liar."

"Then say nothing. We need to get moving, get a head start."

"Okay, let's go," Ribby said. She was out of her mind with worry about Martha. She asked herself how this ever could have happened. She felt so guilty.

At the house, Stephen got into the back seat of the car, and they sped off, leaving Abbey standing in a cloud of dust.

Chapter Sixty-Five

IN THE COLD AND dank waiting room, Teddy paced back and forth like an expectant father. His temper was rising with each and every moment he was made to wait. Sixty minutes. Ninety minutes. One hundred and twenty minutes. No sign of her. No sign of anyone.

Hours later, Teddy heard a clanking noise as the keeper of the keys approached the door. "Excuse me," he said abruptly as the woman passed right by, "I've been waiting in here for hours."

"Mr. uh, Anglophone. At your request I asked for an exception. It was denied. Follow me, and I'll take you back to reception."

He got all up in her face and said, "What do you mean it was denied?"

"Mrs. Balustrade is waiting to be sentenced," she huffed. "Now, I'm a busy woman and it's late so please follow me."

He did as he was told, but he wasn't happy about it.

***

Teddy was still fuming when he got into the limousine. He called The Four Seasons Hotel and booked a suite, then ordered his driver to take him there.

On the way, he speed-dialed Tibbles.

"Tibbles! I need you to get Angela on the line and pronto!"

"She's out for a walk with Abbey. Uh, hold on for a moment." Tibbles cupped his hand over the phone when he saw Abbey enter. He asked her about Angela's whereabouts. Abbey said she and Angela had parted ways hours ago.

"Mr. Anglophone, apparently Miss Angela hasn't returned yet."

"Well *FIND HER*. Ring me back as soon as you know her whereabouts." He disconnected.

"Could you ask Stephen to come in Abbey? It's urgent." Tibbles said.

"I haven't seen Stephen."

"Have a look around the property. Tell him to report to me immediately."

Abbey looked in the common areas of the house. She wandered around wasting time, both inside and outside. Half an hour later, she returned without Stephen. By then Tibbles was about to blow a gasket.

"Where is HE?"

"I looked all around. He's nowhere to be found."

"Do everything oneself. Do everything oneself," Tibbles mumbled. His shoulder connected with hers as he brushed by. "If I find him out there, I will dock your pay by fifty dollars and next time you'll look when I ask you to!"

"But, Sir," Abbey started to say more, but Tibbles slammed the door behind him.

Tibbles also looked everywhere. No sign of Stephen. No sign of Miss Angela. He returned to the house and called Anglophone.

"Tibbles?"

"Yes Sir, it's me. I can't find Stephen or Miss Angela."

"Are they together?"

"I have no idea."

"But surely that girl would know. You told me she was to be Angela's shadow. Put her on the phone."

"She's not at hand."

"What am I paying you for? Find her and put her on the damned phone." Tibbles unhooked the phone and carried it with him. When he heard movement above, he went upstairs.

Abbey was tidying up Miss Angela's night table. She picked up a book with a shadowed figure on the back.

Tibbles entered and thrust the phone into Abbey's hand. She dropped the book and it hit the floor.

"Hello," she said timidly.

"Abbey," Anglophone said, "I need your help to find Miss Angela. It is an urgent matter. Where is she?"

"I left her out walking earlier. She wanted to be alone."

"And Stephen. Did you see Stephen?"

"He was trimming the rose bushes before." Her hands were shaking and her voice too.

"Put Tibbles back on," Anglophone demanded.

"She's lying," Anglophone said to Tibbles. "Find out what she knows and call me back."

"But how?"

"I don't care how. By any means. Find out and NOW!" Anglophone shouted down the line.

Tibbles clenched his fists and stood. He crossed the floor and when he was face-to-face with Abbey, he backhanded her.

The unexpected blow sent Abbey flying backwards and she landed on Ribby's bed. He climbed on top, straddling her and holding her hands and legs. The black polish from his boots scuffed the duvet.

"Tell me!" he shouted into her face. When she wouldn't answer, he held the pillow to her face and let her struggle. He lifted it off again. Her eyes. Soft, like a doe's. "Tell me!" He pushed the pillow down again and she flailed. When he lifted the pillow off, she finally confessed, and he let her sit up and catch her breath.

He called Anglophone who let out a cheer at the other end of the phone. "Well done, Tibbles. Your loyalty will be rewarded."

Tibbles hung up the phone, and then turned to face the young girl.

Abbey remained on the bed, staring at him with those eyes. "Stop looking at me!" he shouted as he pushed the pillow into her face. She struggled a bit at first, but then she surrendered. He kept the pillow pushed in as time stood still.

When he removed it, the girl's eyes were wide open. She looked peaceful. Like an angel.

Tibbles began to shake. He grabbed hold of the night table and noticed a book on the floor. He picked it up, and immediately recognized the eyes from the shadowed figure on the back. They belonged to his master. For a moment he sat, staring at the cover of Everything You Ever Wanted To Know About Black Magic (But Were Afraid To Ask.) His mind wandered to Rosemary and her plea for assistance.

Tibbles opened the flue and started a fire. He tossed the book in and watched it burn.

He rolled Abbey in Ribby's duvet, slung her over his shoulder and carried her body out into the garden. He dug a shallow grave under the rose bushes. After she was buried, he set the roses back where they were, and sprayed a little water onto the garden. It was a lovely resting place.

Back inside, Tibbles showered and tidied himself up. Then he busied himself in Miss Angela's room. He remade the bed with fresh sheets, pillowcases, and new duvet. Perfect.

When he had completed all his duties, the silence became deafening. Even his own footsteps echoed loudly in his ears.

After some time, he could no longer stand the sound of his own breathing. It seemed so loud, so noisy.

He returned to his room and put on the robe Anglophone had once given him. He went into his bottom drawer and pulled out a handgun.

While seated in his favourite chair in his favourite smoking jacket, he blew his brains out.

No one was home to hear the gunshot.

Only the birds were startled by the unnatural sound.

Chapter Sixty-Six

Rosemary Franklin, Stephen's mother, was long gone. She had imagined escaping from the sanitarium, dreamed of it so many times. When the opportunity presented itself, she went for it and climbed into the back of the Clean-it-4-U van. It was 4 a.m. and she was on her way.

The van sped along for quite some time with her hidden in the back. As soon as they were out of the hospital gates, she changed into an outfit she had stolen. She'd also lifted a diamond ring and some coins.

At his first stop Gus, the driver, climbed out. Rosemary watched as he entered the diner. Once the coast was clear she opened the door and ran. She hid beside the exterior wall between the buildings. From there she could watch Gus feeding his face and wait for him to leave. She smelled the wafting pleasant aroma of fresh coffee brewing and bacon sizzling inside. Just the thought of it made her mouth water. So much more tempting than the foul stench of hospital food she'd grown used to.

A door creaked and she shivered as the sun made its way up the sky. Gus climbed up into the van, fiddled with the radio, put on his sunglasses, and pulled away.

Rosemary remained hidden for a few more moments. *Better be safe than sorry.* When the van was clearly out of sight, Rosemary finger brushed her hair. She went into the diner where she ordered a cup of coffee and downed it. The taste of freshly brewed roadside diner coffee was nothing less than heavenly. The waitress came over straightaway and refilled it. The second cup she savoured.

When she was ready to go, Rosemary dropped some coins on the table. She knew she didn't have enough but hoped the waitress would give her a pass. Rosemary burst into tears, sobbing uncontrollably into her hand.

The waitress returned, "Is everything okay dear?"

Rosemary lied. "My husband hits me. I ran away. This change is all I have. I need to disappear. If he finds me, he will drag me back."

The waitress handed her a tissue. "Do you have somewhere safe to go? Or should I call the police?"

"Yes, I have a son, Stephen. All I need to do is get to him. If you could call a taxi and explain the situation, I would appreciate it. I need help in getting away."

"Why don't I give you my phone and you can call yourself?"

"Because my husband will call every taxi firm in the province. If they have my name, he will find me." She sobbed into the tissue again.

The waitress told her she called a taxi, and it would be right over.

"Can I ask one more favour?" When the girl nodded, Rosemary requested a couple of ciggies and a packet of matches. With a smile, the girl obliged.

When the taxi arrived, Rosemary thanked the waitress. "I'll bring my son in here one day to meet you, dear." The young woman smiled and waved, which Rosemary returned.

"Where to, lady?" the driver asked.

"Theodore Anglophone's estate."

He looked at her in his rear-view mirror and nodded.

"On the way, I wonder if you could take me to a pawnshop. I have something I would like to sell. Of course, you can keep the meter running," Rosemary said.

"It's your money, lady. There's a pawn shop along here about twenty minutes away. I'll drop you off and get myself a cuppa and a slice of cherry pie a la mode."

"Thank you very much, Jimmy," she said after glancing at his photo I.D. displayed on the dashboard.

Jimmy looked in his rear-view mirror again. When she flipped back her hair, the sunlight bounced off the rock on her finger. He swerved to avoid an oncoming car. "That's some rock, lady."

"Thank you," Rosemary said as she stared out into the distance.

"We're here," he said.

Chapter Sixty-Seven

Soon the plane arrived in Toronto.

"I need to see my mom," Ribby said.

Viveca called the penitentiary, explaining she had Martha Balustrade's daughter with her.

Access was denied.

"The sentence is being rendered tomorrow at the courthouse. Let's book into a hotel and get a good night's sleep," Viveca suggested.

"Why won't they let me see her?"

"All they told me was the prisoner wasn't allowed any visitors tonight," Viveca said. "What's the nearest hotel to the courthouse?" she asked the driver.

"The Hilton is within walking distance."

Viveca called ahead and booked three rooms. "I'll use my expense account," she said.

They registered at the hotel, agreeing to meet in the lobby. From there they'd head to the courthouse together.

***

The next morning Stephen and Viveca tried to get Ribby to eat something. They managed to get a cup of tea into her but nothing more.

"I'm so glad you could come along for moral support, Stephen," Ribby said.

Angela gave him a wink.

Viveca cringed at the inappropriateness of Ribby's behaviour. She noticed it made Stephen uncomfortable. She paid the bill, and they left the building. The noise in the street was deafening.

"Traffic chaos. Glad we can walk there. Welcome to the city," Stephen said.

They made their way to the courthouse.

Chapter Sixty-Eight

ANGLOPHONE HAD EXPERIENCED A restless night without Tibbles there to manage him. In his absence, Anglophone had called the house. He'd done that before many times. Tibbles was only too happy to help by winding the music box and holding it up to the phone. This time however, he did not answer.

When he saw him next, Tibbles better have a damned good explanation ready. He was fond of the man, but he could be infuriatingly negligent at times.

As he sat awake for hours, he wondered about his son and daughter. Where were they? They must be in the city somewhere. He remembered the two of them making doe eyes at each other. Unaware they were siblings. He too had been attracted to his own daughter—before he knew who she was, of course.

For a moment, Anglophone imagined confessing his paternity to his offspring. He went further, imagining weddings, then grandchildren running around his house, screaming, chasing him. He hated children. Spending all his money. He gave his head a shake, picked up the ugly lamp beside his bed in the hotel room, and threw it at the wall. It shattered, and the lightbulb sparked and then died. There was no way in hell they were ever going to hear it. Not from his lips anyway. He was no family man. Never would be. Family ties created nothing but complications.

He considered Martha's predicament. She had requested his help.

In the morning, he breakfasted in his room. The coffee was unpalatable. He summoned his chauffeur, and they made their way to the courthouse.

Chapter Sixty-Nine

ROSEMARY PAWNED THE RING. Afterwards, she visited a stationery store where she purchased a pen, some paper and an envelope. On the way to Anglophone's estate, she wrote a letter. When she was finished, she sealed the envelope and wrote on the front: "To Stephen Franklin. Private and Confidential." She did not include a return address.

At Anglophone's mansion, Rosemary asked Jimmy to place the envelope into the mailbox. She didn't want to chance running into Tibbles.

"Where to now, lady?"

"The library. I mean Anglophone's Library. Know where it is?"

His head turned. "I can take you there."

"Thank you."

They arrived at the library a short while later. At first, Rosemary remained in the back seat of the taxi with the meter running unable to move.

Jimmy asked, "Is everything okay?"

Rosemary folded her arms around herself afraid to get out. Afraid to be back. Afraid of what she intended to do. "I'm fine," she said.

Jimmy turned the radio on. Crooned along with Elvis.

Rosemary opened her door. She placed a few bills in his hands, "Thank you, Jimmy. You've been wonderful—and you have a rather good singing voice too."

"Thank you, there'll never be another Elvis." He got back into his taxi and sped away.

Once he was out of sight, Rosemary took in the full view of the library. It had once been her favourite place. Her sanctuary. And the air outside still smelled wonderful. The pines, oh the pines. She felt like she was finally free.

That feeling didn't last for long. Soon the bad memories began to whirl around in her head again. Anglophone standing over her. Torturing her. The black magic. Pouring animal blood on her. All for that ruddy book.

Her hands shook as she reached in her pocket and pulled out a bent cigarette. The waitress had been truly kind giving it to her. She lit it and took a long pull. She coughed but continued to take extra drags until her hands settled down again.

More memories resurfaced. Memories she'd been hiding from were triggered like a summer storm. Anglophone using her as a guinea pig. Her threatening to go to the police. Him threatening to kill their son. It had to end, his torture of her. Her threatening to tell Stephen who he was.

A plan was formed then. A compromise. Rosemary would disappear for all intents and purposes and a death certificate would be issued. Since they were married in secret, no one knew she'd changed her name. Stephen would have a job for life, but he'd never know who his father was. Would never know he was heir to Anglophone's fortune. In return, Rosemary would receive the care she needed. Her burns would heal, and all expenses would be covered. To protect her son, she agreed to be locked up for the rest of her life. In theory it seemed doable at the time.

After she asked Anglophone to release her and he'd refused, she had no choice but to escape. Besides, Stephen deserved to know the truth. Rosemary had to be the one to tell him. She sat down on the steps between the library arches and imagined her son finding the letter and reading it. Her mother's intuition told her she was doing the right thing.

Rosemary stood and dropped the cigarette onto the ground. Spent some time gathering materials. Logs, sticks, anything flammable she could find. Whatever she could carry. She put the kindling on the front entryway and set it alight then added the larger pieces. She stood between the wooden arches with her arms open wide and waited for the flames to engulf her.

The smoke would have been visible for miles and miles, but everyone who might have been bothered enough to notice was either away or dead.

The wooden arches caved in before the fire reached Rosemary. While the flames danced in her peripheral vision, the collapsing heavy beams smashed her skull. No more suffering. No more pain.

Chapter Seventy

At the courthouse, Viveca used her Press Pass to get them near to the front even though the court room was jam packed. On the way to their seats, Ribby noticed a few familiar faces including neighbours. She hated the idea of her mother being on trial let alone going to prison.

Let's go outside for a smoke.

No, Mother will be coming in soon.

Big deal. She's not going anywhere.

Ha. Ha.

The atmosphere in the courtroom was out of control. Gossipers were gossiping. Those who had nothing significant to say still added their own two cents. When Martha was brought in, everyone stopped and stared.

The prisoner was unkempt. The grey suit she wore did nothing for her. She'd lost weight. Ribby thought her flame-scarred face resembled a walking corpse.

Geez, even I kind of feel sorry for her.

Ribby sobbed.

Martha looked up at her daughter and almost smiled, but then she looked away.

"All rise," the Bailiff said. "The Court of this Province is now in session. The Right Honourable Judge Delvecchio presiding."

The Judge acknowledged all who were present and sat down. The bailiff indicated that all in the courtroom should do the same.

Ribby looked at the woman who held her mother's fate in her hands. She had kind eyes, even from this distance, and Ribby hoped the woman would show mercy.

"Martha Balustrade, I find you guilty of all charges."

There was pandemonium in the courtroom.

Judge Delvecchio stood and cried out, "Silence!" She fell back into her seat. "I'm ready to pass sentence now." She paused. All present held their breaths.

"Martha Balustrade, you are sentenced to twenty years in prison."

Martha remained silent.

Ribby stood and said, "But she didn't do it."

"Order, order!" Delvecchio said as she slammed the gavel down. "Order or I will clear this court room!"

Shut up Ribby! Shut up!

When there was silence, the Judge spoke to Ribby. "And who are you?"

For God's sake, Ribby shut the fuck up.

"Your Honour, my name is Rebecca Balustrade, but everyone calls me Ribby. I am Martha's daughter."

Voices rang out. More chaos. The judge threatened to clear the room once again. She motioned for Ribby to continue.

Anglophone entered.

"My mother is innocent, and I know this to be true."

Ribby, please.

"And how do you know?" Judge Delvecchio asked.

There was silence for a moment or two, while Ribby clenched and unclenched her fists just like Angela had taught her too.

Ribby disappeared and Angela took over. She rummaged in her handbag, pulled out a cigarette and lit it. She took a drag, dropped the cigarette on the floor and stamped it out. She looked in the direction of Judge Delvecchio.

"She, Ribby, doesn't know anything. *She's so immature that she created me— her imaginary friend— and she's in her thirties. She's had to cope with a lot in her life including living with that poor excuse for a mother.*" Angela turned and pointed at Martha.

The tears rolled down Martha's cheeks.

Angela. No.

Angela continued, *"So, I did the things she wasn't able to do. All of them."*

Everyone leaned forward. She had their full attention. The audience hung on her every word. She felt empowered, like she was in a Shakespearean play performing a soliloquy. She'd never been a fan of the Bard, but Ribby read him. He bored her to tears. "As to the Wheeler person, he was raping Aunt Tizzy. I had no choice. I had to get him off her. He was killing her."

Angela stopped speaking. She turned her gaze first toward Anglophone, then at Martha before turning back toward the Judge.

Her audience had waited long enough. "*I decided to get rid of the body. The plan was to drive him off the cliff in his van. Good riddance to him. He wasn't worth anything more. Tizzy was supposed to jump out of the van before it went over, but she didn't. She went over, too.*"

Martha stood. She attempted to speak, but her lawyer silenced her then pulled her back down into her seat.

"Order! Order!" Judge Delvecchio yelled. "I will clear this court room if everyone doesn't quiet down."

Angela walked over to Martha's table. She poured herself a glass of water. Took a sip, and glanced back at the Judge who said, "We are waiting."

"*I usually don't get to talk very much,*" Angela said. "*Not out loud anyway. It's thirsty work.*"

There was some laughter in the courtroom. Judge Delvecchio becoming impatient slammed her gavel down several times. She stood up and opened her mouth....

Angela interrupted. "*I also confess to the murder of a bouncer on the other side of town. In self-defence, I killed him because he tried to rape me.*"

What? Angela?

You know nothing, Ribby.

Angela paused. "So, here I stand before you. Guilty of everything. I tell you no lies. I did these things, but Rebecca, I mean Ribby Balustrade, is innocent. You see, from early on I could block her out. I could completely take her over. So, if you want to prosecute anyone then you need to prosecute me. Thing is, I don't even exist. I'm not Ribby. I am Angela."

Anglophone stood.

Angela said, "She even lost her virginity without knowing. She still doesn't know."

Ribby screamed.

Anglophone pushed along his row, out and into the centre aisle. He raised his cane into the air and was immediately disarmed and tackled to the ground. As he was dragged out of the proceedings he yelled, "I am Theodore Anglophone!"

No one cared.

"Order In the court! I said order!" Judge Delvecchio yelled as she hammered the gavel several times. When all were quiet, she said, "In light of this new information, case dismissed. Martha Balustrade, you are free to go. A new trial will begin immediately after a psychiatric assessment. Officers, please take Ms. Balustrade down to lockup pending further investigation."

Martha stood with tears streaming down her face, "But I plead guilty. I accept the sentence. Lock me up, please. Let my daughter go."

"Too little too late, Mommy Dearest."

The hammer went down again, and the Judge said, "This is a court of law and we try murderers here, not bad mothers. I could hold you in contempt of court. I could fine you for wasting the court's time. For perjury. For harbouring a murderer. For obstructing justice. Do you get the gist? I advise you to be on your way and let the court do what we must. This court session is now adjourned. Clear the courtroom, bailiff." Judge Delvecchio stood. Everyone else followed and watched her as she disappeared into her chambers.

Martha watched her daughter as the officers handcuffed her and led her away. Angela glanced at Martha over her shoulder and smirked. It was almost as if that glance stopped Martha's heart, or that's the way they told the story afterwards. Martha fell to the floor and expired before the ambulance had time to get there.

Chapter Seventy-One

MARTHA BALUSTRADE WAS BURIED with her daughter in attendance. Ribby was guarded by two officers and dressed in her grey prison garb with her hands and feet bound. The guards placed some flowers in her hands. She tossed them onto the casket as she said her final goodbye.

Isn't that Anglophone's limo?

Yes. I wonder why he's not getting out.

After his performance in the court room, it's surprising he's even here at all.

He hardly knew my mother.

I still have no idea what he was trying to do.

He was lucky they didn't shoot him.

Anglophone was there but chose to remain in his limousine. He did consider getting out a few times and paying his respects. He also considered confessing everything. Rather than face up to things, he ordered his driver to take him home.

He slept a little on the way and as the car drew up to the front of the house, he noticed a bright orange envelope sticking out of the mailbox. After he read it, he tore it to shreds.

Anglophone called his driver back. "Take me to the library."

By the time Anglophone arrived, the fire had burned itself out.

Anglophone looked at the blackened rubble. All that remained of Rosemary. He realized that's why Stephen hadn't been allowed to see his mother. Why he'd been forced to cause such a ruckus at the hospital. The idiots had let her escape. He almost felt bad for docking his pay. Almost. He'd have to call the hospital, get them out here to gather up her bits. They'd cover it up, since he was their biggest donor. Keep it out of the papers. No one would ever be the wiser. After all, Rosemary was already dead. By committing suicide, she had in fact made it impossible for Stephen to ever know who his father was.

Anglophone was shaken up when the chauffeur dropped him back home. He expected Tibbles to be there, to greet him, to comfort him—but there was no sign of his trusted manservant.

"Tibbles!" he bellowed.

His voice echoed throughout the house, but there was no reply. Anglophone was too exhausted to try to find him. He went to his room, wound up the music box and dropped off to sleep for a little while.

When he awoke, he felt a terror go through his soul and he screamed out for Tibbles. He pulled and pulled on the bell so many times that again it dropped out of the ceiling. Still, no one came.

He felt very alone, and he was.

Except for Tibbles who was dead in his own room and Abbey who was buried under the roses.

Chapter Seventy-Two

AFTER AN EXTENSIVE PSYCHIATRIC assessment, Ribby's trial was swift. She was sentenced to twenty years in prison. Ten years for each murder, less time served. Tizzy's death had been deemed a suicide.

Ribby cried non-stop for days which turned into weeks. She was unable to cope in the hostile environment. She was surviving on the edge.

"She's talking to herself again," Ribby's cellmate, Shona said. Shona had been convicted for the murders of her husband and two children.

The prison guard came to assess the situation. He saw Ribby cowling and rocking on her bed. He reprimanded Shona and told her to stop yelling or he'd put her into solitary confinement.

"Aw come on," Shona said. "I didn't do nothing."

"One more word and you are going down to the SHU," the guard said.

Shona stuck her tongue out in defiance as the guard turned his back and walked away. She stood watching him for a few seconds before she turned around and faced Ribby. "I'm watching you, bitch!"

Ribby turned her face toward the wall.

"Don't turn your back on me, bitch!" Shona said as she gave her a shove.

Angela stood, grabbed Shona by the throat. She shoved her against the far wall with a force which caught the cellmate by surprise. Shona's head snapped back. It cracked as it connected with the cold bricks.

With her hands around Shona's neck she said, "*Let me make a few things clear. Number one, you will not talk to me. Number two, you will not touch me. And number three, if you do either of the two things I just mentioned, I will kill you.*"

Shona's eyes were swimming around in their sockets. She tried to respond but gasping for air was all she could do. The woman acquiesced with a nod.

Angela returned to her bed, but before she laid down on the thin mattress, she grabbed some water and threw it in Shona's face. This action snapped the cellmate out of her daze.

Shona spread the word about Ribby. She was a badass not to be messed with. A few others tried, but Angela put them right down. She'd had enough of Ribby's snivelling and victimhood for a lifetime.

Years went by. Cellmates came and went.

Angela remained in full control. She was both respected and feared. In time, she owned the place. It was her prison now and she had control over it and over Ribby. Life was liveable.

Chapter Seventy-Three

AFTER A FEW YEARS, Anglophone made an unexpected visit to the penitentiary. He did not visit Ribby. Instead, he met with the newly appointed prison warden, J. B. Bedford. Bedford was the grandson of an old acquaintance who owed him a favour.

"I would like to fund a library here," Anglophone said. Anglophone was hairless now. His body shook all the time, and he couldn't stand for long.

"That is very generous of you," Bedford replied. "Although to be honest, the inmates could do with donations of many items. I mean, before books."

Anglophone leaned in close to Bedford. "Make a list and get it to me. Money is no object, but a library is a must and quickly. I'm an old man."

"Sure thing," Bedford said. "If you've got the cash, we'll even name it after you."

"No," Anglophone said. "I do not want recognition. However, I would like you to involve one of the inmates. She can help in the creation and maintenance of the library itself. Her name is Ribby

Balustrade. She is a qualified librarian. Of course, I'll donate boxes full of books."

Bedford knew of Ribby Balustrade. She was a ballbreaker who during her stay thus far had risen to the top as the new queen of the pack of inmates. Bedford did not feign his surprise when he said, "She sure doesn't seem like the librarian type."

"Ribby Balustrade is indeed the librarian type. Are we agreed?"

"Sure thing," Bedford replied.

"Oh, and one more thing," Anglophone said. "She must never know about my involvement. I mean, never."

"Got it," Bedford said.

***

When Angela heard the news about the new library she was not amused. Libraries and books were lame. She had worked hard on her reputation. She wanted to keep her status in the prison. She had to keep her profile up. To maintain fear. Without fear she'd lose everything she'd worked so hard for. She wouldn't be able to protect Ribby if she was always swanning around the library.

Reading is positively dullsville and if you want me to protect you, then I need to be in charge here.

Once the prisoners have a library, they'll have something to do. It'll get better.

Oh my God, Ribby, can you be this stupid? Really?

Before the idea of the library, Ribby's personality had been happy to take the back seat. Now it resurfaced. Ribby felt nearly happy.

I'll be able to help others. Introduce them to books. Plus, as a bonus I'll be able to read whatever I want to.

All the time in the world to bore ourselves silly and to put a target onto our backs.

It'll be okay. I know it will.

Wake me up when it's over.

***

Ribby stood in the center of the unused room. It would soon be made into a library. It was spacious enough, but the naked wooden rafters in the ceiling were ugly. So were the cold brick walls and the slate floors. She could fix the walls by covering them with bookshelves and the floors with carpeting. The ceiling though, was another issue all together.

Boxes arrived daily, filled with old books and new books. A few of the crates, needed to be opened with a crowbar. Inside the boxes the books were bound into categories with rope. Ribby filled the shelves, setting everything in order.

When the new library was finished, Ribby stood alongside Warden Bedford. The inmates gathered around for the grand opening. A ribbon cutting ceremony took place.

Her fellow inmates entered in small groups. Ribby showed off the place. She was proud of the tables and chairs, the carpets. And the books, so many books! Not to mention sliding ladders for easy accessibility. One thing they couldn't change though were the wooden beams on the ceiling. They were still ugly, but the lighting helped to hide it.

Most of the inmates reacted positively to the library. Except for Angela.

Ribby, those women are extremely dangerous. It's only a matter of time before they come after us again.

Don't be ridiculous. This library is a game changer.

Ribby's obsession with the new library gave Angela every reason to stay away more and more.

One afternoon, Ribby spoke to the warden about starting a book club. He thought it was a good idea, but as they only had one copy of each book it would be difficult to run a traditional book club. Ribby asked if she could contact local bookstores and ask for additional copies. Bedford tossed her a few coins for the pay phone. It took her a couple of days to get a yes, then a donation of twenty-five books arrived. The very first prison book club book would be Fyodor Dostoevsky's *Crime and Punishment*.

Once the first twenty-five copies were made available, inmates talked about the book. They wanted to read it too. The monthly book club concept turned into a weekly book club. Inmates lined up to join.

When are we ever going to have some fun?

This is fun and we're making a difference. Look at the other prisoners. We're doing something good here.

You are such a goody two shoes.

Why, thank you.

You put the bore in the word boring.

So, go away then. I don't need you anymore.

The warden noticed a huge difference in his inmates' demeanour. He called Ribby into his office. He thanked her for the suggestions. As a new warden he was keen to make his mark, and Ribby helped him to stand out.

He asked if she had any other ideas on how to improve things for her fellow inmates. Ribby suggested author readings. The warden said he knew someone who knew a popular Maine Author. Ribby sent a letter via the warden's friend, in which she mentioned the Book Club would soon be reading *Stand By Me*. Soon authors from all over the world were donating books and asking to come to the prison to discuss their books.

The warden again called Ribby in and asked if she had any other ideas. She mentioned a Family Day when inmates could read to their children. She often watched families together in the meeting room surrounded by prison guards. The children looked too scared to speak. This was ineffective for the entire family. She suggested cordoning off a segment of the library, where one family at a time could read together. The warden thought it was an excellent idea and offered to give it a try. Word of mouth brought in more donations from bookstores. They added a Children's section.

Ribby's next suggestion: to teach inmates who were unable to read to do so.

Next, she requested donations to set up a Job Corner. Computers came in and were hooked up to the WI-FI so inmates could work on their resumes before their release.

Word spread throughout the prison system. Warden Bedford received accolades and awards. He never failed to mention Ribby's contribution.

✳✳✳

A BOX OF BOOKS still had to be unpacked. Ribby cut it open. On the back cover, was a silhouetted man.

Anglophone.

Do you think he did all this? And why didn't we notice it was him before?

I'm not sure, it seems obvious now. I wonder why though, why did he do it?

Guilt? Remorse?

Love?

Ribby was at the top of the ladder, when Angela tightened the rope around the wooden rafter. She made a noose and placed her head into it. When she was ready, she began to chant:

Goody Two-shoes, Goody Two-shoes!

Ribby stood firm. She removed the rope from around her neck.

No.

Angela strained to gain control, grabbing the rope, and once again placing her head in it. As she pushed herself off the ladder, Ribby managed to keep hold of the top rung with one hand. With the rope still fastened around her neck, Ribby hung on for dear life.

Angela attempted to push off again, still humming the tune. The sheer force of it caused Ribby's hand to come loose.

Ribby and Angela hung for a moment, then seemed to fly toward the light. But the rope was not long enough. They pendulummed, then collided with the ladder. It flung sideways and pushed off to the far wall where it landed with a thwunk.

An ambulance arrived too late.

Epilogue

Some years later, a letter arrived from Anglophone's lawyer addressed to Stephen.

In it, the truth was revealed: Stephen was Anglophone's son and sole heir.

"Anything interesting?" his wife, Viveca asked.

"Not at all," Stephen replied as he tossed it into the fire.

The happy couple sat together on the sofa while their daughter Rebecca read a book.

Quote

"Mistress mayoress complained that the pottage was cold;
'And all long of your fiddle-faddle,' quoth she.
'Why, then, Goody Two-shoes, what if it be?
Hold you, if you can, your tittle-tattle, quoth he."
CHARLES COTTON

Word From The Author

Dear readers,

Thank you for reading Ribby's Secret. I hope you enjoyed reading it as much as I enjoyed writing it!

Ribby's Secret first began as a Short Story in 2011. The story ended when Ribby spit into Martha's drink.

It wasn't long before Angela started talking to me. I ignored her, saying the project was finished, but she persisted.

Then along came Theodore Anglophone.

It's 2024 and here we are!

I'd like to thank my proofreaders and beta readers - over the years there have been many. Last but not least thanks to my final editors LF & MC - you two ladies ROCK!

Thank you also to my husband and son, for always being there for me.

As always - Happy Reading!

Cathy

About The Author

Multi-award-winning author, Cathy McGough lives and writes in Ontario, Canada, with her husband, son, their two cats and one dog.

Also by:

FICTION

Everyone's Child

13 Short Stories (which includes: The Umbrella and the Wind; Margaret's Revelation; Dandelion Wine (READERS' FAVOURITE BOOK AWARD FINALIST))

Interviews With Legendary Writers From Beyond (2ND PLACE BEST LITERARY REFERENCE 2016 METAMORPH PUBLISHING)

Plus Size Goddess

NON-FICTION

103 Fundraising Ideas For Parent Volunteers With Schools and Teams (3RD PLACE BEST REFERENCE 2016 METAMORPH PUBLISHING.)

+ Children's and Young Adult books